She was gorgeous. And when she laughed as if she'd burst, she was delectable.

But it was irrelevant. He wasn't interested in finding a woman. Any woman. So it didn't matter what he thought about Evie.

She straightened up, seeking his gaze, and he returned her smile. Suitable woman or not, he was glad she was here.

But he must remember she was here short-term, although thinking that felt like throwing a bucket of cold water over himself. He probably should have done that to himself every night since he'd first seen her, but it was too late now.

He risked a look in her direction and caught her gaze. Then he knew. It was definitely too late.

It didn't matter what he'd told himself; it didn't matter that he wasn't looking for anyone; it didn't matter that he had nothing to offer.

What he was about to do had been inevitable from the first moment he'd seen her. Maybe before?

Emily Forbes is actually two sisters who share a passion for reading and a love of writing. Currently living three minutes apart in South Australia, with their husbands and young families, they saw writing for Medical™ Romance as the ideal opportunity to switch careers. They come from a medical family, and between them have degrees in physiotherapy, psychology, law and business. With this background they were drawn to the Medical™ Romance series, first as readers and now also as writers. Their shared interests include travel, cooking, photography and languages.

Recent titles by the same author:

WEDDING AT PELICAN BEACH

BY
EMILY FORBES

Pure reading pleasure

First published in Great Britain 2007
Large Print edition 2008
Harlequin Mills & Boon Limited,
Eton House, 18-24 Paradise Road,
Richmond, Surrey TW9 1SR

ISBN: 978 0 263 19948 2

Set in Times Roman 16¼ on 18¼ pt.
17-0408-56162

Printed and bound in Great Britain
by Antony Rowe Ltd, Chippenham, Wiltshire

WEDDING AT PELICAN BEACH

This book is dedicated to all the Aunts
in our family, from our Mother's aunts,
to ours and to our children's.

Fel and Nancy, you may see a little bit of
yourselves in this one and although the
Conga-line didn't make it this time, Fel,
there's always another story to be told.

So to all those wonderful women, thank you.

CHAPTER ONE

'NOT again!' Zac Carlisle looked in the direction discreetly pointed out by his colleague, Dr Lexi Patterson.

The trail of disaster left behind by Bob Leeming, the recently 'let go' human resources manager, apparently had one more sting in its tail. A sting that was about five feet nothing and wearing little more than a cropped top and some sort of hip-scarf covered with hundreds of little gold coins, which were jangling as she leant on the nurses' counter, hips swaying to a beat only she could hear.

'A belly dancer? The hospital is falling apart, we're desperate for a nurse and he takes on a *belly dancer?*'

'Shh,' was Lexi's helpful reply. 'She'll hear you.'

And it seemed the belly dancer *had* heard. She turned around, grinning, and the wattage of her smile made him forget about the fact she was the most inappropriately attired nurse he'd ever seen. Until Lexi smothered a giggle and he came to his senses. A gypsy, that's what she was. A gypsy sent to take his already sanity-testing work life one step closer to hell.

'I've gotta run, I need to collect Mollie, but I'll call later, have fun,' she said as she left, leaving him to send the new disaster packing.

The new disaster was walking towards him, holding out her hand, her grin lighting up her face—how could a smile that huge fit on a face that petite and fine-featured, a face like a china doll's?

'I take it you're Dr Carlisle.'

He'd thought she was English—the nurse he was expecting was coming from the UK—but beneath the rounded vowels lurked an Australian accent. She waggled her proffered hand a little, prompting him to shake it.

He did, reluctantly taking her tiny hand in his own—surprised at the firmness of her grip—then releasing it as quickly as he could. A woman who had him thinking about china dolls, gypsies and belly dancers was not a woman to be trusted.

'I'd ask your name but I'm afraid you're going to tell me it's Eva Henderson.'

'No.'

'No?' His luck had changed and Bob Leeming hadn't thrown another disasterous employee in his path?

'Actually, yes, it is, but I prefer Evie.' She laughed. 'And I wanted to see if you'd brighten up if you didn't think I was about to start working here. But I gather I *am* the problem.'

She slipped a hand onto her half-naked hip, just above the scarf-thing which he saw was tied over a barely-there skirt, and although he kept his gaze firmly on her face there was such an expanse of perfect creamy skin on show it was not without effort he resisted a peek. She was tapping her foot, but with impatience or still to the invisible beat she'd been moving to when he'd first seen her he couldn't tell.

'Bob Leeming took you on?'

'You're not going to tell me there's a problem, are you? I mean, I know he's left, but I'm here, and…well, I need the job.'

Large, dark eyes were staring up at him, framed by lashes that were indecently thick and sooty-coloured. He'd like to think the gaze was pleading but he had a bad feeling the mood was more one of confidence. She knew he couldn't send her packing.

'Funny, you don't look like you've come dressed to work.' He was aiming for sarcasm but he just sounded as exhausted as he felt.

'It's the country, I figured we could be more casual here and—' She broke off and patted him on the arm. Presumably she'd seen the look of utter panic that had swept across his face at her announcement—things *were* every bit as bad as he'd guessed. 'I'm joking. Really. I don't start until tomorrow. I just dropped in to visit someone and to finish off my paperwork. See, I am responsible. I'm a day early.'

'I didn't say you were irresponsible.'

'You didn't need to.' Her tone was as merry as his was glum. 'You might just as well have yelled it across the room. It would have fit nicely into the same sentence as "belly dancer"—I think that was the word you used.' She laughed again. 'Sorry, I'm talking too much, I must be nervous.'

'I don't know why you would be. You seem to have made yourself perfectly at home in around ten minutes flat.' Maybe in the next five minutes he'd get a handle on this meeting. Right now he was trying to ignore the thought that Eva—Evie, he corrected himself—was the most extraordinary case of walking, talking confidence he'd ever seen. And just his luck, she'd landed slap bang in the middle of his already enormous pile of problems.

'Who were you visiting? You're not from here.'

'Letitia.'

'My *patient* Letitia?'

'You're her GP?' She considered this for a moment, then looked him up and down without any attempt to be discreet and added, almost to herself, 'Yes, I guess you are.'

He nodded, words seeming less and less possible by the second.

'She's my sister-in-law and— Oh.'

'What?' He looked around for the source of her surprise. 'She's your sister-in-law and what exactly?'

'What exactly?' She took his hand in hers again and shook it with great enthusiasm as she talked. '"What exactly" is that we're going to be neighbours.'

'Neighbours?' He was reduced to repeating her last words.

'I've moved into Jake and Letitia's house so I

can look after their girls when they go to the city for Lettie's surgery. She mentioned how weird it was to live next door to her GP but, as we all know, that sort of thing is par for the course in the country.'

'This is hardly the country.' He'd recovered his powers of speech at last. 'And *you* are hardly a country girl. At least, not from any country I've ever been in,' he muttered.

'Correction. I *am* a country girl. Jake and I grew up in Wagga Wagga.'

'New South Wales? I thought you were English?' But that would explain her curious accent, he could definitely hear an Aussie twang.

'Nope, just been living there.'

He was having trouble keeping up with her conversation, a situation he was unfamiliar with. Her state of dress, or undress, was offputting. And she was still grinning at him. No wonder he was having trouble concentrating. 'Are you always this cheerful?'

She nodded. 'Don't worry, it's not contagious. At least, not unless you kiss me, then you'd have a terminal case of cheer.' She laughed, apparently confident she'd silenced him for good this time, and, waggling her fingers at him in a wave, positively sashayed out of the department and along the corridor.

Leaving him very, very worried that if this was Evie when she was brand spanking new to a place, what would she be like once she'd settled in?

As he watched her almost dance down the corridor he could feel the tenuous grip he had on everything start to slip. But how could a woman who was about as big as Lexi's eight-year-old niece Mollie pose *any* sort of threat to the future of the hospital? Any more of a threat than it was already under.

Why could he still feel the imprint of her tiny hand on his palm?

The questions were coming faster than he could mentally articulate them.

Why would any woman—a soon-to-be-employee to boot—run around a hospital in a be-coined, jangling hip-scarf?

And just how long would it take him to get the image of her swaying hips, curving up to a tiny waist, out of his mind?

'Dr Carlisle!'

Zac, with one hand on his office door, felt his

heart sink at the sound of his name being called. The heavens were conspiring to ensure he never got on top of the administrative nightmare his life had become of late. Thanks to an emergency last night, he hadn't even been able to check Evie's qualifications like he'd meant to. Now it was only eight a.m. and he'd already been here for two hours, delivering a baby who wasn't meant to arrive for another three weeks.

Turning, he suppressed a sigh but couldn't muster a smile. 'Yes, Doris?'

Doris tutted at him. 'You know I wouldn't bother you if it wasn't necessary.'

His smile came of its own volition. 'I know, Doris, but I haven't switched my pager on and I'm not officially here, yet you manage to track me down.' He tugged at his tie, still unfamiliar attire, but he wore it because he couldn't be sure when there'd be an impromptu visit from a certain government department hell bent on dis-mantling the hospital, brick by brick. First im-pressions counted and with a tie on, he rationalised, he had an armour. Of sorts.

'Better than a bloodhound, I know. Lisa and Bruce called through.' She named two of the local volunteer ambulance officers. 'They're bringing in a teenager with complications and they're not sure what they're dealing with. ETA five minutes.'

'Schoolies' week?'

'A fair bet, I'd think.'

'Bloody kids.' He was striding towards the emergency department. 'When are they going to learn that descending on a small seaside town intent on killing themselves isn't the smartest way to mark the end of their school lives?'

Doris was trotting at his side, making a fair attempt of keeping up without actually running. 'They're teenagers. In their minds that makes them invincible.'

He pushed open the doors to the emergency department and stopped in his tracks. Doris, not having any warning, bumped squarely into his back and let out an 'Oomph' of surprise before scooting past. He scarcely registered. He only had eyes for Evie.

Except he'd stopped short because he hadn't been sure it *was* her. Deep in conversation with another nurse, she hadn't seen him. She was dressed in a crisp white nurse's shirt, tucked into a pair of navy trousers, no coins around her waist today. Her dark hair was pulled back and secured tightly at the nape of her delicate neck into some

sort of bun. The image wasn't nearly as disconcerting as the belly dancer of yesterday and he
was conscious of a moment of disappointment.

Then she looked up and flashed her gypsy
smile at him, letting him know his abruptness
yesterday hadn't shaken her confidence. Please,
he prayed silently, let her confidence be justi-
fied. An over-confident, incompetent nurse—
could there be any worse fate for him?

'Good morning,' she sang out, moving towards
him with lithe grace. 'I was getting the run-down
from Libby—'

She broke off as the screech of a siren was
heard in the distance. 'Shall we?' She motioned
to the external door and they fell into step, exiting
the department through the automatic doors out
to the ambulance bay.

Judging by the siren, the ambulance was almost
there and he had no idea what to expect from their
patient, and even less from the nurse meant to be
assisting him. 'Are you equipped to deal with this?'

Had she bristled? He didn't care if she had. He
had a department to run and if he, as one of the
senior staff members, had no time to indulge his
own ego, he sure as hell wasn't about to make
room for hers.

If she had bristled, she didn't take the bait, merely nodded, adding, 'Of course,' in an unflustered tone.

Evie wasn't about to start an argument with Dr Carlisle. She needed this job, and she didn't have time to cater to the ego of Mr Big Shot Country Doctor. That wasn't why she was there and she wasn't going to give him the satisfaction of pulling her up.

But if he'd been trying to needle her he let it drop. Maybe he was just checking, nothing more. Besides, she liked him. First impressions counted, although this morning he looked even more dishevelled than yesterday. She risked a sideways glance up at him, assuming he wouldn't notice as he seemed somewhat distracted. He towered over her, a shadow of a beard darkening his jaw. What time had his day started? It didn't look like he'd had time to shave. His thick brown hair was longer than conventional—was it intentional or was he overdue for a haircut? His blue-grey eyes were solemn and he reminded her of a big shaggy bear, grumpy after a long hibernation, in need of some company, perhaps in the form of a great big belly rub. And she was great at belly rubs. First, though, she'd get rid of that ridiculous tie which he obviously felt uncomfortable in, and—

The shaggy bear's voice broke into her thoughts. 'Today, Nurse Henderson.' Oops.

She didn't even bother with a reply, just hot-footed it next to him as the ambulance screeched into the bay. Zac threw open the rear doors before the driver had turned off the engine and inside the ambulance Evie could see a second officer leaning over the patient.

Zac greeted him. 'Morning, Bruce, what have we got?'

Bruce climbed out of the ambulance and Zac pulled the stretcher towards him, watching as the legs unfolded to support its weight.

'Seventeen-year-old male, complaining of chest pain and stomach cramps. Heart rate 140 and irregular, resps 50 but settling with oxygen,' Bruce replied as he took charge of the stretcher.

The patient had an oxygen mask over his mouth and nose and Evie could see a saline drip running into his arm. A portable oxygen cylinder and a drip stand were attached to the stretcher.

'Apparently he had hallucinations of some sort

and became aggressive and then confused.' Bruce continued to talk as he pushed the stretcher through the hospital doors. 'We're assuming he's been drinking and has perhaps taken drugs or a mixture of drugs. We're told he vomited, but the kids aren't telling us much more so we're working blind.'

'What's wrong with these kids? Does someone have to die before they'll see sense?'

'At least one of them thought to call us, but it would help to know what we're dealing with.' Bruce's tone was calm in contrast to Zac's frustration.

Evie hurried alongside the stretcher, guiding it to a stop inside the first examiation cubicle. Fortunately the emergency department was empty at this hour of the day and she didn't waste time drawing the curtains—she wanted to start treatment. The patient was in a bad way. Very bad.

'What's his name?' she asked Bruce, not bothering to introduce herself. There'd be time for that later and if he was going to fuss he could read her ID tag.

'Stewart.'

Evie leant over the boy, shaking him gently by the shoulder. 'Stewart, can you hear me? You're in the hospital.' She pulled up his eyelids as she spoke and that got his attention. He lashed out at her, knocking her arm away. She wasn't hurt but cursed herself for not reacting faster.

Stewart pulled off the oxygen mask and continued to thrash about, swearing and yelling. His pupils were dilated, his breathing shallow and rapid.

'Grab his arms, he needs restraints.' Evie caught Stewart's left arm, just before he managed to rip out his IV line. 'My money's on crystal meth,' she said as she clung to Stewart's arm with all her strength, gratefully aware that Bruce had pinned Stewart's other arm.

'Pardon?' Zac's voice came from the foot of the stretcher, where he was trying to hold Stewart's flailing legs. Stewart was doing his best to connect and, despite his size, Zac was struggling to contain him.

'Crystal meth, methamphetamine—you know, ice, speed. He's got all the right symptoms of an overdose.'

'Do you *know* that, or is it something you've seen on a TV show?'

Evie decided to ignore the jibe. It wasn't her fault she knew more than he did. 'I know you don't know me, but I know what I'm doing.' She let go of their patient's arm as Libby finally tied a restraint around his wrist, fixing him to the stretcher. Replacing the oxygen mask on Stewart's face, she continued, 'I'm from *London*. This is like a common cold there.'

He looked at her a fraction longer through narrowed eyes, his expression unsure. She didn't have time to go into further detail. She needed to take a blood sample and drawing blood from an eighty-kilogram moving target wasn't easy. Libby had fastened the other straps and fortunately Stewart gave up the struggle once he was restrained.

'What if it's not drugs? What if he's had a fit?' Zac asked.

'It's possible,' she conceded, 'but I'll bet my first pay packet it's drugs. I'll take blood and we can get it tested.'

'We can't do that here. Bloodwork gets sent to Adelaide. We're a small-town hospital, we don't have all the services you're used to in London.'

He had no idea what she was used to, she thought. She wasn't always in London and she'd worked in far more primitive conditions than Pelican Beach. But now wasn't the time to have that discussion—their patient was her priority.

'If you can do an EEG, that might give you some info but if it was a fit it's over and the treatment plan would be virtually the same.' Evie popped a tourniquet around Stewart's left biceps and slipped a needle into the vein in his elbow as she spoke. 'Until we contact his parents we've no way of knowing his medical history. He's not wearing a medic-alert so I'm with Bruce. I think we should treat it as a drug-related problem.' She was watching Zac—creased brow, blue-grey eyes—who looked torn between believing her and telling her to get out of the department.

Something lifted in his expression. Had practicality won out?

'What do we do?'

'Stabilise him, monitor him, rehydrate him. Sedate him if necessary. The effects of ice are made worse by lack of sleep and lack of food. My guess is they've been partying all night. Stewart needs to be rehydrated and sedated while the drugs wear off.'

As Evie finished speaking, a policeman entered Emergency and Zac, after nodding in her direction, which Evie took as permission to start treatment, left her side to talk to the officer.

She enlisted Libby and Bruce to transfer

Stewart to a hospital bed then Bruce was free to go. Libby and Evie worked in harmony to retie the restraints, attach a new bag of saline to the gelco in Stewart's right arm and connect him to the monitors. Evie started a chart and filled out an order for a sedative, ready for a doctor's signature. She placed the chart at the end of the bed, turned around—and collided with Zac. For a tall, solidly built man he moved awfully quietly. His hands shot up and he held her arms, steadying her.

'You OK?' He dropped his hands, but not before she knew she'd have preferred it if he hadn't. 'When you've finished, Bill would like a word with us both.' Evie glanced over to where the policeman was waiting. 'It seems the kids have been buying drugs, ice included.'

So she'd been right—nice to know, at least from a professional point of view. She stopped herself from saying 'I told you so' because it was suddenly important for him to like her.

She crossed the room, holding out her hand. 'Bill, I'm Evie Henderson.'

Bill shook her hand. 'Welcome to Pelican Beach. Sorry about the circumstances.'

'Not a great start, for me or Stewart.'

'How is he? Lucky to be alive?' Bill asked.

'I think he'll be OK. You've spoken to the other kids? They were taking ice?'

'Smoking it, apparently, but they weren't too forthcoming with the information. Scared, I reckon, but I think they were more frightened by not knowing whether Stewart was dead or alive.'

'It's pretty rare for ice or speed to cause heart failure or to stop respiration.'

Zac shot her a dark look. 'Are you condoning the habit?'

'Of course not, but we all need to understand the drug and what we may have to deal with. The deaths associated with its use have usually been attributed to people inhaling their vomit and drowning. In the light of the fact you've got… how many kids descending on the town?'

'Thousands.' His tone was grim.

'I think we need to find out whether Stewart has taken the drug before. If he has and he's had a psychotic episode previously, it increases the likelihood of it recurring. But if he hasn't taken it before, or hasn't had this reaction, then you may have a problem with the quality of the drug and Stewart won't be our last customer. Someone has to tell us about Stewart's drug history and we need to get hold of the rest of the batch. Even better, find the supplier.'

'We're onto it.' Bill handed Evie a piece of paper. 'Contact details for Stewart's parents,' he said and then he left with Zac, leaving Evie to get back to day one on the job.

And back to wondering how to get a certain tousled-haired, harried-looking doctor to chill out and accept her. Just enough to be friends. Friends was what she needed. Friends, plural, but she sensed a challenge in Dr Carlisle, and she wasn't one to back away from a challenge.

She had two months, give or take, before she returned to her semi-nomadic existence. Two months was long enough for all sorts of things.

One never knew where life would take you but you could always enjoy the ride. Would Dr Carlisle be prepared to get on board?

Somehow Evie was in control of the situation.

Zac didn't know whether to be pleased, surprised or annoyed. He watched as she checked Stewart's drip and listened as she spoke quietly to her patient, even though he wasn't responding. He realised he had no grounds to be annoyed with her. She was doing her job and doing it well. Was that the problem? That she was proving him wrong in no uncertain terms?

He owed her an apology. But he didn't move, he just stood there, watching her. There was something about her, an energy, a vibrancy that demanded attention. His attention. He had dozens of other tasks waiting for him. So why couldn't he drag himself away?

Evie looked up from her patient. 'Did you want something, Zac?' An encouraging smile showed him she wasn't irritated.

'Do you need me to sign for anything?' He said the first thing that popped into his head.

'Could you sign for a sedative?' She held out the medication chart, indicating where she needed his initials. 'He really just has to sleep this off but we need to contact his parents. Would you call them?' She dug in her pocket and retrieved the piece of paper the policeman had given to her. 'I'm sure they'd prefer to speak to a doctor in the circumstances.'

Even Bill had figured Evie was in charge of the situation but Zac knew she was right. Stewart's parents would expect to hear from a doctor or the police. But he hadn't dealt with this before. What were the specifics?

'It could take a few days for the drug-related chemicals to break down so he'll have to be admitted.' Had Evie picked up his uncertainty—was she feeding him information? Or had she judged his ability, like he'd judged hers, he thought. He didn't like the idea. 'Tell them you'll speak to them in greater detail when they get here.' She glanced at the paper. 'They have an Adelaide address. I assume they'll drive down.'

She held out the paper and he automatically took it. She obviously had things under control and didn't need him. Raising a hand in farewell, he left her to it, busy with his thoughts.

So much for judging a book by its cover.

Which was what he'd done. One look at that hip-scarf and bare midriff and that's exactly what he'd done. He should be pleased—if what he'd seen so far was any indication, Evie was competent. That meant one less problem for him to sort out. He should be pleased. He *was* relieved, but the flip side was he'd been shown up. And that didn't feel so good.

'Is everything OK?' Libby's return interrupted Evie's musings.

'Yes, he's stable.'

'I heard Bill say it was drugs.' Evie nodded. 'If this is how things are going on day one of schoolies week, we could be in for a busy time.'

'You'd better tell me what to expect this week. It sounds a far cry from the quiet coastal life I was promised.'

'With a bit of luck we've seen the worst of it but you have arrived at our busiest time, luckily for us. Schoolies is a bit of an institution. Thousands of seventeen- and eighteen-year-olds "invade" us after their end-of-year exams and sometimes it seems as though all they want is the chance to run amok. There's been trouble in the past with underage drinking, sexual assaults, driving under the influence but we haven't had a drug problem before. I guess it was only a matter of time.'

'And medically speaking?'

'Mostly it's nothing out of the ordinary, just the number of people through the door increases. A task force was set up this year by Max Stoppard, our police chief, who wanted to look at ways to control the crowds. The locals have a bit of a love-hate relationship with schoolies week. It's a good money-spinner for a lot of local businesses but a nightmare for most permanent residents in terms of the kids' behaviour. Max had a mini-conference with the principals of a lot of the schools whose pupils come down here every year and also spoke to the mayor and the publicans.'

'What was the verdict?'

'For the first time there's going to be an organised party in the park on the foreshore, with bands and entry by ticket. The idea was to get the kids into one place to make it easier to supervise. Just enough supervision to let the kids know their behaviour is being monitored, which hopefully lets them celebrate safely. It's an experiment.'

'When's the party?'

'Tomorrow night.'

'I hope Bill has time to get a lid on the drugs issue otherwise we could have our hands full,' Evie said.

'I think they have some contingency plans in place, but I'm not sure if they counted on starting the weekend off with an overdose. Did Bill say what they'll do now?'

'He's going to try to get more information from the kids—we need details—and Zac's gone to ring Stewart's parents.' Evie hesitated but curiosity got the better of her. 'Tell me, is he always so sombre?'

'Zac?'

Evie nodded.

Libby shrugged. 'He's a serious type of person, I suppose. He's got a lot on his plate right now. He takes it all to heart, which is good for the hospital, probably bad for him.'

'What's he dealing with?'

'He's just joined the hospital board and I gather there's a bit of politics going on. I'm not sure why he put his hand up for the responsibility. When I work him out, I'll let you know. But as long as we're doing our jobs, and doing them well, he'll be happy.'

Libby's opinion was cut short by Zac's return.

'Were your ears burning?' Evie quipped. He looked horrified to think they'd been discussing him but didn't ask questions. How long would it take him to lighten up? She guessed he'd run a mile if he had an inkling as to where her thoughts lay.

'I've just spoken to Stewart's parents. They're on their way here and should arrive in a couple of hours.' He had his 'serious' face on again. She was positive he'd have a great smile if she could coax one out of him. 'I've given them a few details but I've left any further questions for when they get here.'

He'd addressed this to both women but then Libby excused herself and it was just the two of them. He seemed a little uncomfortable, but not in a hurry to leave.

'I owe you an apology.'

'You do?'

'The previous HR manager had a knack for putting the right people in the wrong jobs and vice versa, and employing some absolute disasters. It took me a while to sort all that out. I jumped to conclusions when I first met you and I'm sorry. I questioned your ability as a nurse. I've been put straight.' He spoke earnestly, as though it was a matter of grave importance and he anticipated a blast. 'I apologise.'

'Apology accepted,' she said graciously, although she hadn't given two hoots. 'I guess I was lucky my first patient wasn't a shark-attack victim. I don't know how impressed you would have been then. Overdoses I've had plenty of experience with, sharks—not so much,' she said, smiling, and expected a smile in return. But, once again, nothing.

Her two-month time limit suddenly seemed a bit ambitious. Zac looked like he might be a hard nut to crack.

Evie was beaming at him and he found himself completely disoriented. Her smile was like a beacon, drawing him closer. He shook his head, trying to clear his mind, aware he was staring but unable to turn away. He tried to focus on what she'd said. Overdoses. That was it. Something about being familiar with overdoses.

'You did a good job. Stewart was lucky you were here,' he said, before he bade her goodbye and left the department, as fast as decently possible. Getting away from her distracting smile, away from thoughts of narrow waists, dark hair and large, expressive eyes. Eyes that looked as though they'd seen a lot and had liked most of it.

What had she seen? he wondered. And what had her experience with drugs been? Personal or professional? She hadn't made that clear and there was a lingering doubt in his mind. Was there more he should know?

He had to check her references and her credentials. He couldn't afford to make any mistakes, especially now. He'd judged her too quickly the first time—but he'd better make sure he wasn't leaning too far the other way, on the strength of one good performance, especially with Bob Leeming's terrible track record.

He hoped her past was clean. She'd be good to have around.

Good for the hospital, he clarified, that was what he'd meant. They could use her skills.

Unbidden, an image of Evie floated into his mind, her shimmering scarf-like skirt shifting around her thighs, jangling with gold coins as she moved with a lithe step. The image, so free, so *care*free, it mocked the beleaguered mood that had been his constant companion of late. Resentment he hadn't known he had burned inside him. She was the epitome of everything he'd *thought* he was. Only now he was finding out his life must have been a lie because, just a few weeks into his new role, he couldn't even keep up the appearance of being on top of his job.

He'd hesitated today with the drug case, and it didn't sit well. She'd sailed right in there, no hesitation, no doubts. What did that show? That he'd lost his nerve, just when he'd needed it most?

He reached his office and opened the door, marching to his desk and yanking his chair out to sit down.

No, he hadn't lost his nerve. All he needed was a few extra days in the week. And a benefactor with pots of money to get the hospital out of its predicament.

The hospital might benefit from her skills but there was nothing a belly-dancing gypsy with an incredible smile could do for him.

Nothing that didn't spell trouble, and he already had enough of that.

CHAPTER TWO

EVIE stitched and bandaged, disinfected and swabbed solidly for another two hours before Libby sent her for a break with words of encouragement ringing in her ears. She was desperate for a coffee but would there be a stash of condensed milk in the staffroom? That was the only way to drink it, two-thirds deliciously rich, totally addictive condensed milk with an inch of thick black coffee dripped on top. So thick the spoon could almost stand up by itself. Yum. Zac thought she'd been condoning drug-taking but coffee was her only vice and, as far as she was aware, it wasn't illegal. Although if she didn't get her condensed milk hit this side of lunch, she might well commit an illegal act.

'Lettie!' She shoved open her sister-in-law's hospital room door and flopped into the chair at her side. As there wouldn't be condensed milk, there was no point wasting her time with a coffee-break. 'Resting after your five-k run?'

'Sure, a brief respite then I'm off to the gym. Me and my trusty wheels.' She motioned to the wheelchair parked nearby.

'And here I thought you were faking it.'

'Don't I wish.'

'Any news about a transfer?'

Letitia shook her head, a wave of dark straight hair shifting across her shoulders. 'But now you're here I'm ready to go.' She reached out and took Evie's hands in her own. 'Thank you so much for coming back for us. You have no idea what it means to us and we know what you've had to give up—'

'Rubbish.' She cut Lettie off. She didn't need another tirade of thanks. 'It took me a second to decide and I can pick everything else up when you're back here, bossing my brother and two gorgeous nieces around again.' Which wasn't quite true. Being torn between two causes was an experience she didn't want to repeat any time soon, but there was no way she'd tell Lettie that. The whole martyr-thing wasn't her style. 'Speaking of which, I hope you know I have no intention of feeding my nieces vegetables while you and Jake are gone.'

'You love vegetables!'

Evie shook her head. 'That was just a cover until I got the gig of looking after the girls.' She'd successfully, if underhandedly, distracted Lettie by introducing one of her pet loves: discussion of her children's diets. Being married to the hospital chef and working in the kitchen herself, balanced diets were a favourite topic of conversation and seeing children with poor diets could send her right off. 'Secretly, I'm a hot chips and sauce girl. Besides, you won't be able to chase me when you're flat out doing your rehab. And, you should know, I'm intent on becoming the girls' favourite aunt while their parents are gone.'

'You're their *only* aunt.'

'All the more reason I shouldn't make them hate me by forcing them to eat their greens.' She glanced at the watch pinned to her shirt. 'Gotta run. I don't want big bad Dr Carlisle eating me alive on my first day for being late back from a break.' Lettie was making a strange noise. 'What? Are you choking? I was just joking about the veg—' Then she realised and, turning slowly towards the door, felt a laugh rise up in her throat.

Big, bad, *shaggy* Dr Carlisle was standing in

the doorway. And from the look on his face, he'd heard every word she said. Oops again.

'Um, just so you know, that's Letitia's name for you, not mine.' She couldn't help it, she knew it wasn't funny, but she giggled.

'Evie!' Her sister-in-law's tone was scandalised.

'Letitia, I have some news for you.' He paused, looking pointedly at Evie.

She took the hint—it was hardly an obscure one—and stood, bending down to drop a kiss on Letitia's cheek. 'Don't give the nurses too much grief.' Heading for the door, she added, 'I'll pop back on my lunch-break.'

As she passed Zac, she heard him say softly, 'She'll be looking forward to it, no doubt.'

Was that exasperation or a hint of amusement in his voice? She slowed her steps to peer up at him but his gaze was so inscrutable she'd need a jackhammer to get at any hidden meaning. And a ladder to get a close-up view.

'How tall are you anyway?'

'Pardon?'

She really, really hadn't meant to say that out loud. 'Nothing.' Three strikes and you're out? Was that how things worked here? She didn't stick around to find out and, speeding back to the emergency department, made a vow to come down from the high she'd been on since arriving. She hadn't realised how much she'd missed her family and although she was here because of Letitia's condition, and although she still felt sick at how she'd let down the project in Vietnam—the children!—part of her was euphoric about being here. What a pity Dr Carlisle was in such furious disagreement. If she couldn't change his mind then being rather un-welcome on that front might take the gloss off her stay a bit, and if that didn't, the reality of juggling shift work with the care of a six- and a seven-year-old could well sink in some time in the next few weeks.

She thought of the small box sitting in Letitia's kitchen. Twenty just wouldn't be enough. This was easily a fifty-tin mission. But did Pelican Beach stock enough condensed milk to see her through?

And just what would Dr Carlisle say if he got wind of her addiction? She didn't know him well—or at all, really—but she just *knew* he wasn't one to tolerate addictions. Of any sort.

Libby popped her head into the examination cubicle where Evie was checking Stewart's obs.

'Zac's here with Stewart's parents. They'd like to see him.'

'OK, just stall them for a minute while I untie these wrist restraints. I'll leave the ankle ones on, they're covered by the sheet, but I don't want them to see him tied down.'

'What if he lashes out again?' Libby sounded nervous.

'He's pretty heavily sedated, we should be OK.' Libby nodded and ducked out as Evie untied the straps. She'd just put them into the bedside drawer when Zac appeared.

'OK to come in?' Zac waited until she nodded, then drew back the curtains to admit Stewart's parents. 'Evie, this is James and Helen Cook. This is Sister Henderson, she's been looking after Stewart.'

James shook Evie's hand but Helen, after giving her a brief nod, headed directly for Stewart's bedside. She picked up his hand and began talking to him before turning to Evie, a look of concern on her face.

'Is he sleeping or is he unconscious?'

'He's had a sedative. He was quite distressed and he needs to rest.'

'Why is he still in the emergency department?'

'Stewart needs close monitoring and Evie has the most experience with these cases. He'll be transferred to a room when he's stable, but it was best to keep him with Evie,' Zac explained.

Of course, once they heard she was the expert, all questions were directed to her.

'Is he going to be all right?'

'We won't really know for a few days until the drug-related chemicals are cleared from his system but, physically, he should be fine. Emotionally it might be a different matter.'

'He's never done anything like this before. I don't understand it.'

'Truth be told,' said Stewart's father, 'we'd probably be the last to know if he has been experimenting with drugs.'

James was right but Evie wasn't about to say that out loud. Helen was shaking her head.

'No, his behaviour has been quite normal, even with the pressure of final exams. I'm sure this is just a one-off.'

'It's quite possible this was his first experience with methamphetamines. I imagine the kids are quite easily persuaded to experiment a little in a party environment like this. But one of the problems with crystal meth is that it's highly addictive. People have become addicted after one hit.' Evie paused to let that sink in. 'Stewart is going to need counselling and education and he's really going to have to be watched to make sure he stays away from drugs. You can't pretend this hasn't happened and you can't afford to think it was a one-off. I've seen how quickly people become addicted and what a mess it can make of their lives. The most dangerous thing you can do is to pretend it won't happen again.'

'What can you tell us about crystal meth—is that what it's called?'

'Yes. You've probably heard of "speed" or "ice"?' James nodded. 'Speed is the powder form of the drug and ice is the crystal form. Because the drug is illegal, there's no control over the formula and no control over the amounts kids take. They can snort it, inject it or smoke it, although I didn't see any evidence that Stewart has injected anything into his veins.'

Helen looked horrified at the image Evie described but James stayed focussed. 'What effect does it have?'

'Most take it for the feeling of euphoria and increased energy it gives. It can increase alertness, meaning kids can stay up all night. Some girls use it as an appetite suppressant. The drug and alcohol centre will give you a lot more information. The best thing to do is make an appointment for you to go as a family. They'll answer all your questions and if you do it together, you all get the same information.'

'When will I be able to talk to him?' Helen asked.

'The sedative will wear off later today but once people come down from the high they're usually exhausted and can sleep for the better part of a few days. I wouldn't expect to get much sense out of him until after the weekend. We'll move him to a room later this afternoon and you're welcome to sit with him, but don't expect too many answers. I'll leave you with him now for a few minutes. Call if you need anything.'

'We will,' they replied, and she left them, turning to acknowledge their thanks as she left the room.

Would this family be able to pull Stewart through? Would there be a happy ending? She'd seen too many cases where that hadn't happened but she didn't have long to dwell on that thought before another case came through the doors.

At least one problem he'd woken up with had been resolved.

He'd gone to sleep with some lingering reservations about Evie and had woken up knowing he had no reason to doubt her. It had just been his bruised ego whispering in his ear.

She'd proved herself and for once Bob Leeming had stumbled on a competent employee. Ironically, now that he'd fixed the mess left by Bob, the only position he had to fill before handing personnel issues back to the HR manager was the position of HR manager. He had two interviews lined up over the next few days and his fingers were firmly crossed that one of the applicants would be suitable. Then he could officially hand the whole thing back where it belonged.

He checked his desk clock. His long day was nearly over, just a board meeting to get through. It was scheduled to start in thirty minutes. Half an hour to pull a miracle out of his hat. He needed a miracle if they were going to find a solution to the funding crisis that was threatening the hospital. Zac cursed the state government for their narrow-mindedness. Why were the rural communities always being short-changed to benefit their city cousins? Zac knew why this government was proposing to decrease funding to rural health services but it didn't mean they had to accept it without a fight. There had to be a way around this, but he couldn't seem to find it.

Two heads might be better than one. He picked up the phone to dial his fellow board member and GP, Tom Edwards, not that their discussions about the hospital's future had got them anywhere so far. Married to another of his colleagues, Lexi Patterson, the couple had become his good friends since he'd moved to Pelican Beach.

Twenty-five minutes of brainstorming got them no closer to solving the crisis facing the hospital, but it almost made them late for the meeting. Two hours of frustration later they left the meeting together, both more dejected than when they'd started.

'Beer on my porch?' Zac asked, although they were already cutting across the hospital lawns towards his house, the beer a foregone conclusion. 'Has Lexi given you a leave pass?'

'Absolutely. Her favourite programme is on so she prefers it when I'm not home on a Friday. Apparently my wisecracks at the expense of the extraordinary stupidity of the characters offend her sensibilities. Can't think why.'

'Why, indeed.'

Tom pulled up short as they reached Zac's front gate. 'It's not home brew?'

'What's not to love about my home brew? But, no, I haven't had the time lately. Cooking is the only relaxation left to me.'

'Then we're still on.'

Tom took a chair on the front porch while Zac went inside and within a minute was back again with two cold bottles of beer. Flicking the caps off, he passed one to Tom before taking his seat and settling into the evening darkness, both men content to sit with their thoughts for a while after the stresses of the day.

Taking a long draught, Zac looked across the front garden towards the hospital, its windows lit up, faint noises drifting back to them on the warm, scented evening air. The hospital was less than a hundred metres away, and the staff accommodation, a few hundred-year-old row cottages, were in its grounds. Great in some respects but it meant he was never really away from his work. If the on-call doctor couldn't be tracked down, he was all too available.

Into the peace came another sound.

His new next-door neighbour.

Evie.

She'd come out of her front door—all of three metres from where they were sitting—and was seeing a visitor off. He couldn't see her over the stone wall dividing their front verandahs but her voice, surprisingly deep for someone so tiny, was soft and smooth.

He stilled, the beer halfway to his lips, as he listened.

'Bye, and thanks again. It was a great night. My place next week?'

The voice of her visitor was low and muffled, not clear like Evie's, and he couldn't hear their side of the conversation. Evie called a last farewell and he heard her door close behind her, heard her footsteps as she walked down her hallway. Had she just had a date? Annoyance, plain and simple, rose in his throat. She'd only just arrived and she seemed as settled in as he was. More so, because, despite Lexi's best efforts at matchmaking, he didn't date.

'Lexi?' Tom was off his seat, calling out into the semi-darkness of the path in front of the cottages.

'Tom! Don't freak me out like that.'

Both men left their chairs and walked down the front path.

'What are you doing here? I thought you were at home, watching that show.'

Zac opened the gate for her and the three of them went back to the verandah, Lexi insisting she didn't need a drink and Zac insisting she have his chair.

'I'm just as happy on the front step,' Lexi replied, before turning to Tom. 'And as for you, *that show,* as you call it, happens to be Evie's favourite, too, although she's a season ahead, coming from the UK. We thought it'd be fun to watch it together. Mum's home with the girls,' she said, referring to baby Erin, her daughter with Tom, and her orphaned niece Mollie, whose guardian she was. 'Evie's nieces are fast asleep. We've had a good night. She's lovely, very funny. Don't you think?'

She'd directed this last query at Zac. He nodded. 'I don't know her very well yet but, sure, she seems nice enough.'

Tom chuckled. 'Nice enough, he says, but he hung on her every word when she came outside just now. She even got his mind off the hospital crisis for a moment.'

'Really?' Lexi said, and Zac cursed Tom for bringing this down on him. Now he'd be under scrutiny from Lexi every time Evie's name was as much as mentioned. And, other than a basic physical attraction, there was nothing to tell. Period.

'You think you might be interested?' And there she went, straight on to the possibility of hooking him up with Evie. 'You'll have to hurry, she'll be heading back to the UK once Jake and Letitia get home.' She paused, obviously scheming. 'But if you fall madly in love, maybe she won't go.'

'What *is* that rubbish you watch on TV, honey?' Tom was laughing. Sure, he could find this amusing, the scrutiny wasn't directed at him. 'My guess is he's just relieved Evie doesn't have three heads, like some of the other staff Bob took on.'

'Thanks, mate, but it's too late to close the stable door now. Your matchmaking wife has well and truly bolted.'

'Then again,' Tom added, 'Evie is hot.' Lexi shot her foot out and kicked Tom in the shin, not too gently either. *Good shot,* thought Zac.

'She is, but you're married, you're not allowed to say that. Zac, on the other hand…' She paused dramatically, waiting for his answer.

'If I agree she's nice-looking, will you drop this?' Nice-looking! If she bought that, he was better at bluffing than he'd thought. Nice-looking didn't come close. *Hot* didn't touch it either. Neither word captured the elusive quality about her, a quality he was yet to identify.

'No, I won't. Why don't you take Evie out while she's here? It'd be good for both of you.'

'Because, right now, my life is crazy.'

'Crazy with work,' Lexi agreed, 'which is all the more reason to make time for pleasure. You should come and picnic with us outside the concert tomorrow night. It'll be fun.'

'Lex, when Zac says he doesn't have the time, believe the poor guy, OK? You know I've been flat-chat lately, double that for Zac.'

He could almost hear the cogs turning in Lexi's brain as she weighed up Tom's words. 'How is the hospital situation looking?' she asked Zac.

Being married to Tom and being an attending GP at the hospital, Lexi was one of the few people beyond the board to know the situation.

'The staffing issues are at least under control. You had me worried when you first pointed Evie out, but she's highly competent.'

'Sorry.' She grimaced. 'I'd heard from Letitia she was a great nurse but I shouldn't have teased you like that.'

'It's OK. Choice of clothing aside, she proved herself pretty quickly. But as for the funding issues, they're not going away any time soon.'

'How'd the meeting go tonight? What's going to happen?'

'At this point, we don't know,' said Tom. 'But the pressure is on to take some fairly drastic measures, beat the government to it so we can show we've taken big steps to cut overheads. And the options aren't pretty.'

'The options aren't options,' added Zac. 'We have to find other solutions.'

'Unless we have a miracle, Zac, the options are the *only* options. And top of the list is the nursing-home.'

'You'll close it?' The horror was clear in Lexi's voice.

Zac stood in one swift movement, anger at the situation pulsing through him. 'Over my dead body,' was all he said.

He could sense Lexi shooting a look at Tom, querying his reaction.

'Zac feels reasonably strongly about this.' Tom's voice was mild, making his words seem even more of an understatement.

'A decent society doesn't neglect the young, the

sick, the disenfranchised or the old. We're starting with the elderly here but, guaranteed, the government will work its way down the list, cutting funding to the groups that need it and can defend themselves least.'

Lexi came over to him and wrapped him in a hug, saying all the right things to show her support.

'Thanks,' Zac said. 'It'll work out.'

'It will. We'd better head off but will you come to the concert tomorrow night? Just for a while? We can pretend we're young again and find out what's cool in the music world nowadays.'

'As long as there are no emergencies, I will.'

Lexi pulled him in close for another hug before accompanying her husband out the gate. Zac watched them leave hand in hand, two people who fate had brought together again after misunderstandings had torn them apart for years. Their laughter lingered, just like the warmth of Lexi's hug on his skin.

The touch of a friend was always welcome, but for some reason tonight it left him feeling sad. Or was it the sight of his two friends so happy together that threw into even sharper relief the loneliness that lurked beyond the frenzy of his life?

Once it had looked as though life was going to turn out differently. Three years ago he had been married and expecting his first child, now he was alone in a country town, overworked, underpaid and with no prospects of anything other than the occasional hug from a friend.

The dreams he'd shared with his wife had turned into a nightmare. His life hadn't been easy but he'd thought he'd found his perfect partner, yet their love hadn't been able to withstand the pressure they'd faced and their relationship had shattered like glass they moment it had been stressed.

People made all sorts of promises in good faith but he'd learnt the hard way that people often weren't as brave or as strong as they'd like to be, and he included himself in that category.

Once he'd risked everything for love—he wouldn't make that mistake again.

This was his life now. Relationships were not for him.

CHAPTER THREE

THE sound of Arabic music pounding from the nursing-home common room was not what Zac expected to hear. It caught him off guard and he paused, one hand flat against the door, ready to push it open. OK, not pounding exactly, but it was hardly the normal volume for the golden oldies channel. He could take a guess at what he might find on the other side—did he need to go in and make his day worse? He hesitated, then entered. Gingerly. As if something was waiting to bite him.

'And shimmy, two three four and shimmy, basic Arabic, forward, hip lift. Left, right and back, two, three, four, shoulder shimmy, and change.'

He sidled up to Pam, the diversional therapist, and whispered, 'What's going on?'

'Evie's entertaining the troops.' She didn't take her gaze off Evie, as transfixed as the twenty residents, who hadn't even noticed him enter the room. Evie hadn't noticed him either.

'We don't have enough cardiac equipment for this. Look at them! Half of them are ready to go into arrest with the next whatever you call that hip...' His attention caught by the movement, he couldn't formulate the words. He tried again, 'That...hip...'

'Wiggle?' Pam supplied, the amusement in her voice clear. Since Evie had arrived, there'd been far too much amusement at his expense. Which was not what he needed right now, with the future of the hospital resting partially on his shoulders.

Evie turned and her gaze landed on him, her smile broadening immediately as if challenging him to interrupt her. She shimmied her way towards the back of the room where her nieces were sitting, as mesmerised as the rest of the crowd.

'*Now* what's going on?' Zac muttered.

'You missed the best bit. She did a proper dance, now she's just been taking the residents through the routine, breaking it down into parts,' Pam replied. Evie's nieces had taken the floor now, and were shaking their non-existent hips and holding their skinny arms aloft in various poses in line with their aunt's instructions. 'This is the G-rated part of the show—Gracie and

Mack are doing their thing, they're just learning. Pretty sweet, isn't it? Look, they have mini-hip-scarves just like Evie's. Dear little things.'

'Poor Letitia.' Zac shook his head. 'What will she say when she gets home to find Evie has turned her daughters into delinquent gypsies?' Except Pam was right, Gracie and Mack *were* adorable. But Evie wasn't just giving instructions, she was still dancing, too, and from the look of the crowd, while the women might be oohing and aahing over the children, the men hadn't taken their eyes off the aunt.

'Silly, that's how Evie and Letitia met up again. They'd been at school together, and a few years later Evie was back for a holiday, and they were both doing a dance class. Letitia only stopped because of her hip trouble.'

'This whole performance needs to stop. Mr Louis is going purple.' But Zac knew it was from excitement rather than exertion. Evie was having the same effect on him. Sure, the girls looked gorgeous but their aunt? Their aunt was a walking advertisement for natural Viagra. Again, exactly what he *didn't* need in a nursing-home. 'How long is this scheduled for?'

'Shh.'

'Egyptian fifth, now turning in full circle, hip lifts all the way. And pose, Egyptian sixth, and hold, two three, four—and that's it!'

'Praise the lord,' Zac muttered as Pam left his side to check on the residents and Evie headed for the CD player to switch it off.

The applause was thunderous and was accompanied by a few wolf-whistles of appreciation and at least two walking sticks being thumped enthusiastically on the floor.

As the initial noise subsided, the room was still abuzz with the over-excited chatter of twenty octogenarians. A group, he saw now, that included his great-aunt Fel and her best friend, Nancy, both of whom were always in the thick of whatever fun was to be had here. He took a step in their direction but was beaten to it—Gracie and Mack had already run to them, one girl clambering onto each lap as though it was their natural place in the world. And from the smile on the older women's faces, they agreed.

A light touch on his arm told him the delinquent gypsy was at his side. She was beaming up at him, glowing from the dancing.

'Hi there.'

'Hi.' A master of the English language he

wasn't, but what did you say to someone who one minute was a nurse working with utter professionalism and the next was decked out in bright orange silky stuff, fringed all over with gold beads of some sort, shaking her booty for all it was worth? And from what he'd seen, it was worth quite a significant amount.

She was chatting away at his side. 'It's not usual, to do a lesson like that, but as I don't have a dance troupe at my beck and call, I can't put on a full-scale show. This seemed like the next best thing.'

He recovered the power of speech. 'Perhaps that's a good thing. I don't think the Pelican Beach nursing-home could withstand a full-scale show.'

'No?' She mulled this over for a moment before peering at him more closely. 'You don't have an issue with me doing this, do you? I gather things can get a bit monotonous.'

He considered her question. Did he have an issue with it? The image of twenty smiling faces swam into view. 'As long as no one has a cardiac arrest, no, I don't. Monotony *is* a problem but we don't have the resources…' His sentence tailed off. He'd been so distracted by her he'd almost forgotten why he'd ducked into the home in the first place. Monotony was insignificant compared to the other problems facing the nursing-home residents. It was just that no one knew it yet. No one except him and the board, which left him feeling more like a traitor every second—but what choice did they have? He changed the topic. 'I don't suppose you have any more sedate talents? Yodelling? Knitting?'

The shine in her eyes increased a degree. 'Put it this way, if I were a Miss Universe entrant, I wouldn't have to think too hard about filling in my special talents section on my form. This is it. I couldn't even whip up a soufflé for the judges, and as for baton-twirling, I'd be liable to knock someone out.'

He laughed and, although it sounded a little rusty, even to his own ears, the troubles of the day slipped back a little. 'If you were a Miss Universe entrant, soufflés and batons would be the least of your problems.'

'Why?'

'You'd be spending all your time avoiding being stepped on. You'd only come up to the other contestants' knee-caps.'

'That's size-ist, even if you are right.' She

tried to look affronted. And failed miserably. 'I'm an uncoordinated, culinary-challenged shrimp. So I have to dance for my supper.'

'What's it called, anyway? Harem dancing?'

She rolled her eyes. 'The ancient art of Oriental dancing. Popularly known as belly dancing, a term I know you're familiar with,' she said with a grin. 'Lots of different styles fall under the name. I do some of them.'

He rubbed at his jaw, aware a sparkle had come into his own eyes in response to the light in hers. 'Like I said, harem dancing.'

She laughed. 'You're such a bloke. You all think it's for you but…' she winked at him '…it's a secret weapon.'

'How come?'

'If I told you, I'd have to kill you. Probably with a hip lift.' She gave him a demonstration, her hips moving as though they were separate to her upper body. With difficulty, he kept from staring. She was right. If she ever did that in private for a bloke—*for him*—it would finish him off.

'Those things should come with a written warning.' He shoved his hands deep into his pockets and nodded at the general region of her hips. He couldn't risk a closer look, he might never drag his eyes away. 'They're lethal.' He sounded like he was joking. He wasn't.

'You see?' She nodded vehemently, and if she knew the effect she was having on him, she was keeping an impressively straight face. 'The secret weapon. When a dancer does this…' she bunched up her hair, holding it on top of her head, all scrunched and messy with tendrils falling down over the smoothness of her shoulders '…and this…' she shimmied around in a circle, whipping her head around so she scarcely lost eye contact with him '…men can't talk.'

She stopped as suddenly as she'd started, grinning. She'd proved her point and she knew it. 'So men think it's for them but, really, when a woman dances, a man doesn't stand a chance. And as for becoming empowered in one's femininity, there's nothing like it.' She tilted her head just a touch on one side. 'You should try it,' she encouraged. 'When you can talk again,' she added, her expression a picture of innocence.

He ignored that, even though she was more than half-right. He had to concentrate to talk. He didn't want to place a bet on what he'd go to sleep envisioning tonight. If the image would *let* him sleep. 'Can I ask you a favour?'

'Sure.'

'Please, don't *ever* do that little number in here without a cardiac unit on standby. And so you know, our public liability insurance doesn't cover death by a belly-dancing nurse.'

'Ah.' She nodded, her face straight again. 'But I was watching Mr Louis, among others, and I'm pretty sure he was thinking, "What a way to go".'

He groaned. 'Tell me you didn't just say that.'

'Say what?' She laughed. 'I'll catch you later. I'm helping Pam with morning tea.'

Didn't she ever stop? She, like his great-aunt, always seemed to be in the midst of things. He glanced towards his aunt. Gracie had left her lap and was now sprinting across the room with her sister, their little hip-scarves jangling all the way. Evie waited beside him while her nieces ran over.

'Hi, Dr Carlisle!' they chorused, and Gracie added, 'That was fan-tas-ta-losa, awesome fun, Evie. Can we do it tomorrow?' Both little girls were bouncing up and down like wind-up toys, their eyes shining bright like their aunt's.

The image struck a chord with him. *That* was what Evie reminded him of—she still had that childlike enthusiasm about her, that glow that told a thousand stories. She lived in the moment.

When had he last stopped and savoured a moment? He was usually knee-deep in all the problems of the future. The thought of how he was nowadays, contrasting so greatly with how *she* was, made him feel, oh, about a thousand and three.

From across the room, an ear-splitting whistle rang out, bringing him back to the present. He'd done it again, forgotten to be where he was, letting his mind drag him off somewhere else he didn't need to be.

'Evie, darling, promise me you'll spare an old bloke a thought and come dance again.' It was Mr Louis, one of the gentlemen who'd been particularly vocal about his appreciation during Evie's performance. 'That was as much fun as I've had since the war!'

'And you've got as much chance of dating this dancer as you had back then,' called his sparring mate, Wilf. 'Buckley's and none.'

Evie raised a hand over her head and waved, making a big show of ignoring Wilf. 'Thanks, Mr Louis. I hope you're not going to let me down for the Big Night Out concert tonight. Pick me up at seven?' she said, sending a huge wink in the old man's direction.

She was a flirt, no doubt about it, but one with such charm she could get away with it. 'Thanks a million, Evie,' Zac muttered dryly. 'You've finished him off for sure, just thinking about it.'

But what he was really thinking was how Wilf would rate Zac's own chances of asking Evie out on a date.

Blast Lexi, she'd put the idea into his head last night.

And blast Evie, too.

There was one thing he did know, having seen her dance today, he had next to no chance of erasing the image of her bejewelled hips moving in a motion all their own, hair loose and streaming down her back as she wiggled and shimmied to the frenzied beat of the music.

Evie wandered over to the refreshment table to help Pam pour the tea, but couldn't stop herself from observing Zac out of the corner of her eye. He said goodbye to the girls as they ran after her but he didn't leave immediately, as she'd expected. She watched as he crossed the room to chat briefly to the two old ladies on whose laps Gracie and Mack had made themselves so at home. He was smiling at the women and Evie marvelled at how his smile lightened his demeanour. It was a great smile, just as she'd suspected. His laugh, too, when they'd been discussing her lack of talents, had taken her by surprise, but in a good way. The serious, almost forebidding expression he normally wore had been replaced by one that implied he might once have known how to have a good time. Evie was sure he'd almost smiled at her when she'd first noticed him in the room and she was determined to get him to do it properly. It was worth it.

He bent to help the women from their seats before kissing them both on the cheek. Not normal behaviour for medical staff by Evie's reckoning, and definitely not what she'd expect from a man as reserved and in control as Zac was. Who were they?

She wasn't left wondering for long.

'Welcome Evie. I'm Felicity and this is my dear friend, Nancy,' said the taller of the two women as they approached the refreshment table. 'Two cups of tea, please, and why don't you join us when you're finished here? We love a new face.'

'Gracie and Mack, choose some morning tea and come with us,' Nancy suggested.

The girls didn't need to be asked twice, quickly piling a selection of sweet things onto a plate before trotting off to a table with the women, leaving Evie to finish pouring tea as she scouted the room for Zac. There he was, deep in conversation with Matron. They made their way out of the common room, still talking, and Evie felt a moment of disappointment when he didn't seek her out as he left. Choosing not to dwell on that thought, she headed to her nieces, put her water glass on the table—there wasn't any condensed milk so coffee was out of the question—and pulled out a chair. Grace and Mack were busy devouring their scones, which was keeping them quiet but Fel and Nancy made up for the girls' silence.

'You're here to look after the girls while Letitia's out of action?' Fel asked.

Evie nodded. 'You know her?'

'Absolutely. She's our favourite dinner lady and we all love the girls.'

'I can see they feel quite at home here.' Evie smiled.

'Any news on when Letitia will be having her operation?'

'Not yet.'

'Imagine having to have two hips replaced before you're forty,' Nancy remarked.

'I'd have thought it would be you or me, yet here we are, over one hundred and sixty years between us and still going strong.'

'And learning how to belly dance, no less. That was the most fun we've had in ages.'

'Since the time we tried to chat up that nice young physio who Zac organised to talk to us about exercise or some such.'

'Remember how horrified Zac was with us!' Nancy giggled.

'He needs to let himself go a bit, he's far too serious. Takes after my brother. And look where his serious nature got him—stress put him into a early grave.'

'Your brother?' Evie wasn't sure if she was following the conversation.

Fel nodded. 'Zac is my great-nephew, my brother's grandson.'

'I didn't realise he had family in Pelican Beach. He's not from here, is he?'

'No. He grew up in Adelaide but his family has a holiday home here. He arrived a few years ago, he needed a change of pace.'

'A change of pace?' Evie sipped her water, trying to conceal her curiosity.

'He went through a nasty marriage break-up,

although that's not common knowledge. He's kept his own counsel.'

'How is that possible in a town this size?' Evie asked.

'People won't pry when it's made clear it's not welcome. They accepted him into the community but they haven't interfered. He knows everything about everyone, he's very good at listening, but he doesn't give away much about himself.' Fel explained. 'People adore him but you ask anyone what they know about him and I bet the details will be sketchy. He plays his cards very close to his chest. He's immersed himself in work and that's become his life now. But I still think he needs a good dose of the scallywags. I bet even Zac can't remember when he last had any fun.'

'Maybe we can persuade him to join us for one of your belly-dancing sessions, Evie,' Nancy suggested.

'You will do more?' Fel didn't sound as though she was used to taking no for an answer.

Evie smiled. 'I plan to, but right now I need to get the girls home to get changed. Their dad's taking them to the beach.'

Evie ushered the girls out of the nursing-home and steered them along the footpath towards their house on the other side of the hospital. Halfway home they ran into Bill.

'Evie, I was just looking for you. Could I have a quick word?' He looked at the girls and back to the Evie. 'Alone, if possible.'

'Girls, why don't you go over to the rose garden and pick some flowers to take to Mum while I talk to Bill?'

The girls skipped off and Evie motioned Bill to a garden bench where they could talk as she kept an eye on her nieces.

'What's up?'

'I've got more information about the drug Stewart was smoking and I want to pick your brains, if you don't mind.'

'Go ahead.'

'It *was* ice. We've been able to test the batch Stewart's hit came from and apparently it was about seventy per cent pure.'

'How did you get some to test? Did the kids hand it over?'

'Not directly. Would you believe one, or more, of them contacted a lawyer and the lawyer dropped the drug off to us. Protecting their own hides, more afraid of what would happen to them if they were caught with the drug than of what would happen

if they smoked it. Unbelievable. We're more concerned with where they got it from.'

'Did the lawyer tell you that?'

'Apparently the kids bought it off some guy
down here.'

'Which means there's probably more about the
place, sold to kids with no idea what it can do to
them.' Evie frowned as she watched her nieces,
skipping between the rose bushes. They were a
picture of innocence but who knew what the
future held for them? For any of them.

'Exactly. If they'd brought it to town with them,
it might not have such an impact, but if it's being
sold in Pelican Beach, we really need to track
down the source. We've spoken to a couple of
small-time dealers but the drug of choice down
here has always been marijuana and, more
recently, a bit of ecstasy. The drug squad thinks
it might be someone from out of town, taking ad-
vantage of schoolies week to make a quick buck.
They're sending a team down to investigate but
I wanted to ask you what we should be doing in
the short term. It's the big concert tonight. This
is all unfamiliar territory to us and to the ambulance staff, too—they're only volunteers.'

'From a medical point of view, you'll need

people who can deal with any repercussions after the drug's been taken. I spent time yesterday putting protocols in place for the emergency staff at the hospital to follow, but there's not enough time to train up the local ambos—can you get some city crews sent down for tonight, crews who'll have experience with this?'

'We should be able to organise that. I'll make sure it happens.'

'I'm sure word'll be getting around the streets about what happened to Stewart but it won't keep everyone away from drugs, especially as kids will be drinking—they'll be more likely to engage in other risk-taking behaviours. Realistically we have to be prepared for more cases like Stewart's and I think calling in experienced reinforcements is your wisest choice.'

'So the hospital team know what to do?'

Evie nodded. 'Yes. But having city paramedics on the ground here is a priority.'

'OK. I'm on it.' He stood and shook her hand, a big, serious man with a lot on his plate. Very similar to Zac in that regard, but he didn't invoke the same shivers of attraction in her that Zac did. 'Thanks, Evie.'

'No problem. Let's hope for the best.'

'And expect the worst.'

'Probably wise.'

Bill left, his worried expression still in place, but at least he had a plan.

As did she.

Look after her nieces and let Jake and Letitia head to Adelaide with no concerns.

Work hard but leave time for fun, too.

Preferably with a particular doctor who'd got under her skin when she'd not expected it.

She might have teased him with her hip lifts earlier, but she had an uncomfortable feeling it would be her, not him, lying awake tonight with a tingle of longing, aching to be satiated.

What was a man to do?

A man needed an evacuation plan in the event of situations like this.

If he could get out of his kitchen, he would, but part way through cooking dinner was an awkward time to make a run for it.

Then again, one more minute of listening to Evie's singing would do permanent damage to his ears. He'd been trying to block all thoughts of her out of his mind but was finding it impossible. And her 'singing', for lack of a better word for it, wasn't helping.

For the last half an hour, she'd been belting out hit after hit at the top of her voice, the sound carrying with ease to him from next door. But sung so appallingly that, despite his ears being assaulted, it was sort of charming. In a way. And maybe for three minutes, not thirty.

He'd seen her talking to Bill on the hospital lawns. Seen her sit with him on a garden seat, and although he knew they'd been discussing work—Bill had spoken to him next—he'd been surprised by the sensation the sight had evoked in him. He hated to admit it, it was unreasonable and he didn't do unreasonable, but he'd been jealous. Annoyed with himself, he'd tried hard to think about other things, and there were plenty of other problems to occupy his mind, problems that didn't involve a tiny, vivacious, belly dancer. But it wasn't working and now she was pushing her way into his consciousness and evoking other visions, other visions that just weren't going to happen. Couldn't happen. There was only one solution, bar deserting his meal and sprinting to the nearest restaurant.

It took all of five seconds to leave his stove,

turned down to simmer, and reach her front doorstep, knocking loudly so she'd hear him above her din.

Gracie answered. 'Hi, Dr Carlisle.'

He squatted down to her level. 'Hi, there, Gracie-girl, your aunt is singing.'

The little girl with dark, dark hair, like her aunt's, nodded solemnly. 'She's making dinner. Daddy is at the hospital with Mummy.'

There went his plans for restoring peace and quiet. They were already covered for food. Which should make him happy—soon she'd be eating and there'd be no more singing. So why did he feel disappointed?

Gracie slipped into the circle of his arms and nestled against his knee. She dropped her voice to a conspiratorial whisper. 'She's not very good at it.'

'At singing? I can hear that.'

Gracie shook her head earnestly. 'At cooking. We have to tell her what to do. Mack is helping, I'm hiding, that's why I heard you.'

'Is that right?' He made a show of mulling the news over, fighting back a chuckle. 'I thought your aunt loved vegetables—doesn't she know how to cook them?'

'She has them *raw.* Yuck.' She giggled. 'She eats bunny food.' She sniffed the air. 'Your dinner smells yum.'

He snapped his fingers. 'I have a plan. Hop on.' He swung the little girl around on to his back and stood, Gracie tapping him on the shoulder to get him moving.

Cantering down the tiny passage, a mirror image of his own, the terrible singing voice increased in volume until he pulled up short in the kitchen doorway. Mack saw him and waved but Evie, in little more than her underwear, had her back to them, belting out another tune, oblivious to the fact her audience had just increased.

He was almost lost for words—she was every bit as gorgeous under her hip-scarf as he'd imagined. He did the right thing and cleared his throat to let her know she had company. She screamed at the noise, her hand flying to cover her mouth as she flung the spatula across the room and looked around wildly, presumably for the nearest thing to cover herself with.

'It's not your mouth that needs covering, Evie, it's the rest of you.' He knew he shouldn't, but the next moment he'd thrown his head back and was roaring with laughter. 'Don't you *ever* wear clothes?'

She seized a teatowel and held it spread out in front of her abdomen. 'I started out wearing clothes, but I spilt sauce on me.' She indicated a sodden pile of clothes in the corner of the kitchen. 'And I wasn't expecting visitors,' she added pointedly. 'What are you doing here, anyway?'

'I've come to extend a dinner invitation. To all three of you.'

Her eyes lit up with hope. 'Now?'

He nodded. Gracie, still clinging to his back like a little monkey, let out a whoop of excitement and Mack added, with a touch of relief, he thought, 'That's a great idea!'

'Really?' That was Evie.

'Truly.' Maybe even madly.

'Can you cook?'

He looked at the pots and pans strewn around the kitchen, none of them appearing to hold anything edible. 'Are you really in a position to ask that?'

She followed his gaze before nodding emphatically. 'You're right. When shall we come?'

'It's almost ready, you can come now if you like. Although you might be more comfortable with some clothes on.' She didn't answer so he added, 'The fabric things you drape over yourself to give the appearance of modesty.'

She grinned and jiggled the teatowel. 'What do you call this?'

'Can Mack and me go with him now?' asked Gracie.

'Mack and I,' Evie corrected her, before shrugging her shoulders, giving up on the grammar lesson. 'Sure, if it's OK with Zac.'

'No problem. We'll see you there.' He swung Gracie down to the floor and beat a hasty retreat back the way he'd come, girls in tow. He'd stopped the singing but now he was going to be tortured with sights instead of sounds. Not that the sight of Evie standing with her back to him, almost every curve of her tiny body revealed, could be called torture. But it would distract him even more than the singing. How was he going to get through the evening? How was he going to pretend he wasn't attracted to her?

Did he want to pretend?

He thought about that as he swung his front door open to let the girls in, and by the time he'd closed it behind him, he knew. It wasn't a matter of want, it was a matter of there being no other option. He didn't do unreasonable and he didn't do foolish. And thinking about kissing Evie was pure madness.

* * *

It had only taken her a minute to pull some clothes on, grab a couple of necessities, leave a note for Jake and walk the few steps down the tiny garden path, out the front gate and back up the matching path to Zac's front door. She'd done her best to appear unflustered but was 'mortified' too strong a word for her colleague seeing her almost naked?

She giggled. She wasn't mortified, not in the least. The disbelieving expression on his face had made any fleeting embarrassment worth it. She'd thought about spending a *little* more time getting ready—but what was the point of fussing over her appearance when he'd just seen her in her underwear? She raised her hand and knocked at his door. When he answered, pulling back in welcome, wiping his hands on a clean towel, she noticed there wasn't so much as a splotch on his white T-shirt or pale linen shorts. He still looked good enough to—

'Almost done.' He ushered her inside, breaking her train of thought. His gaze was on the objects she was carrying. 'What have you got there?'

'My specialty, coffee with condensed milk. I thought I'd make you one after dinner.'

'Sounds good. Come through. The girls are setting the table, you've got them well trained.'

She shook her head, stepping in behind him and following him to the kitchen. 'It's the other way around, isn't it, girls? After tonight I think they'll be begging to fend for themselves at mealtimes.'

'Much safer.' Mack giggled. 'We've set the table—can we play with your world globe?'

'Sure.' They scampered off into the adjacent living area. 'They love that thing,' he said. 'Just out of interest, how are you planning on not poisoning them while their parents are away?'

She sighed. She hadn't been joking when she'd said dancing was her only talent. Tonight was the proof. 'Jake already has the fridge and freezer well stocked, but I thought I should give it a shot while he was still here. Just in case I burnt the house down or something.'

'That bad, huh?'

She shuddered. 'You have no idea. It was *terrifying.*'

'Perhaps you should leave it to the experts.' He was lifting pot lids while he spoke, stirring, testing, pretty much behaving in the same expert manner as her brother. She'd always loved watching Jake cook—she blamed him and their mum for making it unnecessary for her to learn. But she'd never imagined she could watch anyone cook for hours and not tire of it, yet that was her first thought as she watched Zac. And it wasn't just because she and the girls were running the risk of starvation or weeks of take-aways. 'You'll need the bomb squad in just to clean up the mess you've made.'

Yup, even insulting her, he was delicious. She pulled a face at him anyway, and he laughed, lifting a steamer lid and starting to serve.

Sidling up, she took a peek at dinner, peering in through the glass lids of the pots. It looked delicious. A man who could cook—there was something very attractive about that.

He gave a little nudge with his hip to move her out the way and turned off the stove. 'When you've finished snooping, you can dish for the girls.'

'I'm impressed.'

'That I knew you were snooping?'

'That you can cook. Sometimes I think I might be the last remaining person on the planet who has no skills in the kitchen.'

Zac's smile was lopsided, full of cheek, his

arms crossed loosely over his chest as he leant back on the bench, serving spoon in hand, considering her. 'I'm sure you have a plethora of skills in the kitchen, they just don't involve cooking.'

She laughed. 'Now you're getting suggestive.'

'Absolutely.' He nodded, the dark light in his eyes sending a thrill through her. Where was this conversation going? 'For instance, I can't wait to see how skilled you are at cleaning up after dinner.'

Ah. That was not the direction she'd been hoping for. He was holding the two children's plates out to her, laughing as he waited for her to take them.

'You're in the presence of genius, buddy. I can load a dishwasher like no other woman in Pelican Beach. And that's a promise.' She took the plates and banished all thoughts of things other than dish-washing happening in his kitchen. Wretched man, to put crazy images in her head then refuse to follow through! She'd banish all thoughts of Zac, too, but standing so close to him, that was impossible. He smelt delicious and he had some serious charisma going on. She shivered as she brushed against his side, his touch sparking warm, sugary responses in her.

Thank goodness for the distraction of Gracie and

Mack—that was all she could think as they all made short work of the food, seated around Zac's plain kitchen table, laughing at the girls' comments and stories about school and life in general.

All too soon Evie heard her brother's voice calling from the front door. Gracie and Mack made a dash for the door, Zac close behind. Evie followed them, heard Zac offer Jake a coffee, listened to him refuse.

'It's time to get these two buttons off to bed. Thanks…' he nodded at Zac '…for feeding them. You'll keep an eye on them? Throw them the occasional crust if my sister forgets? She's passionate about the world's needy, I'm just afraid it'll be my two who *are* the needy by the time Letitia and I get back from Adelaide.'

Zac laughed, Evie poked her tongue out and Jake winked at her before scooping Gracie up onto one shoulder before she could dash off back down the hall.

'Gee up, Daddy,' Gracie said, holding on around her dad's neck as he bent again to attempt to lift Mack onto his other shoulder. 'Humph,' he said, his voice muffled as Gracie's arm slipped too high and covered his mouth. Letting go of Mack, he tugged Gracie's little arm lower.

'Yup, you're a strong boy, Daddy, but not strong enough,' Gracie said, as Evie fought a stitch in her side—she'd spent too long tonight trying not to laugh. Gracie was going to be the death of her in the next couple of months. 'Looks like we'll have to get a stronger boy here.'

'Are you going to give your aunt this much cheek when Mummy and I are away?'

Gracie considered. 'Yes.'

'That's OK, then.'

Gripping his errant youngest daughter with one arm, he managed to swing Mack into position and left cantering like a pony back next door, the girls squealing their delight and experimenting with holding onto their father's neck with only one hand.

Leaving Evie able to give in to her laughter and Zac half laughing, half watching as she doubled over in the doorway.

She was gorgeous.

And when she laughed like she'd burst, she was delectable.

Her only flaw was that she couldn't sing a note.

It was irrelevant.

He wasn't interested in finding a woman. Any

woman. So it didn't matter what he thought about Evie.

She straightened up, tears in her eyes, seeking his gaze, and he returned her smile. Suitable woman or not, he was glad she was there.

'My nieces are a hoot,' she said when they were back in the kitchen and she could talk again.

'They're going to miss their dad and mum. They're lucky to have you. Letitia told me you were coming to look after the girls so we could organise her surgery, but she didn't tell me you'd be working at the hospital. Was there a reason she kept that quiet?'

'I guess she had other things to think about. I was coming, that was the main thing. The job was secondary and if I hadn't got it, I would've come anyway. We would've just needed a miracle so I could support us all as Jake won't be able to work while he's with Letitia.'

'I knew there were problems but Letitia wouldn't elaborate, just kept saying she could go when you got here.'

She considered, her head tilted a little on one side. 'Too proud to tell you, I guess. They can manage without Letitia's wage, just, but not Jake's. Jake insisted on being with her and we all think that's wise. Letitia tends to be anxious at the best of times and even more so about this situation. Plus they don't have whatever insurance covers you for being sick but not when it's not terminal.'

'Trauma or income protection?'

She nodded. 'Someone needed to go with Letitia, someone needed to stay with the girls.' She ticked off the 'someones' on her fingers. 'And someone needed to earn money to pay for it all. I'm the last two people,' she added with a flourish.

'You're not big enough for two people. Aren't there other family members who could help out?'

'There you go again, selling me short.' She sent him a wink that had him grabbing plates and scraping the contents with unnecessary vigour into the rubbish. She cleared the rest of the table, chatting as she stacked crockery into the dishwasher, oblivious to the effect she had on him. 'Mum and Dad will come as soon as they can, but they have to sell their roadhouse business first. They can't just shut it down and leave, they can't afford to do that. If I won the lottery,' she added, her voice full of cheer, 'that'd solve everything.'

'Your parents own a roadhouse? A restaurant and a garage for truckies, that sort of thing?'

'Absolutely. On the highway heading into Wagga Wagga.'

'They're selling up for Letitia?'

'They were thinking of it already, planning their semi-retirement, and Letitia needing bilateral hip replacements made their minds up. But these things take time. Once they're here, I'll head back.'

He stopped in mid-scrape, the dish at an angle over the rubbish bin.

He'd known she was here short term but hearing it from her felt like she'd thrown a bucket of cold water over him. He probably should have done that to himself every night since he'd first seen her, but it was too late now.

He risked a look in her direction and caught her gaze, dropping the pot onto the kitchen counter, scarcely mindful of his actions.

Then he knew. It was definitely too late.

It didn't matter what he'd told himself, it didn't matter that he wasn't looking for anyone, it didn't matter he had nothing to offer.

What he was about to do had been inevitable from the first moment he'd seen her shake those hips.

* * *

He was looking at her strangely.

If she hadn't known better, he was looking at her like she was kissable and he was planning on doing something about it.

Her toes curled in pleasure at the thought, fictitious though it might be.

There was only one way to sort fact from fiction. Absentmindedly, she touched her lower lip with her tongue then caught it between her teeth, biting gently, just for a second.

If it was true, she'd be reaping her just, if short-term, rewards for putting her life on hold to come back here.

Stepping towards him, she was half-aware of a smile playing about her lips. She was aware, too, of just how absorbed he was by her mouth. His gaze hadn't left it.

He was absolutely still, watching her come to him, and she saw the darkness in his gaze deepen, his breathing quicken. Then she was standing in front of him, so close that, even without the look of desire she knew was in her eyes, there could be no question of what she wanted.

With a groan, he reached for her and pulled her swiftly into the circle of his arms, half lifting her from the floor, her tiny frame no obstacle to sweeping her closer and closer still, until she was pressed hard against his torso.

Her eyes fluttered closed in anticipation but his mouth didn't close over hers. 'Evie.' There was a catch in the depths of his voice.

'Hmm?' She peeked out through her lashes, reluctant to break the spell.

'This wasn't what I had in mind when I invited you over.'

She licked her lips again. 'Is it what you have in mind now?'

'The only thing.'

'Then there's no problem,' she whispered, raising her mouth up to his, eyes closed again. This might not have been what he'd had in mind, but there'd been a good part of her mind that had been occupied with exactly this since she'd first seen him. 'Kiss me already.'

There were no further arguments, no further attempts to do the sensible thing.

He did what they both wanted, bent his head to hers and kissed her like there was no tomorrow.

CHAPTER FOUR

HE WOULD have kept on kissing her if the front doorbell hadn't rung. Then rung again. And again.

They both pulled away, as reluctant as each other to break the magic of their kiss.

He didn't want it to end. Ending it meant he'd have to remember all the reasons he couldn't do this, when all he wanted was to keep on kissing her, for hours if possible. Could he forget the outside world, forget rational decisions for one night?

Evie was glowing. Gorgeous. How could one kiss be enough?

Couldn't he forget his resolutions? Just for a moment in time? Just while she was here? Or even just for tonight? Then his mobile began to ring, too. The outside world wasn't going to grant his wish.

Dropping a kiss on the tip of her nose, he stepped away, missing the call on his phone, and went to see who was still pressing the doorbell.

'Tom!' Damn, he'd forgotten his acceptance of their invitation to the Big Night Out.

Tom shoved his mobile back in his pocket. 'Your house isn't that big, mate. What were you doing?' He motioned to the street. 'Lexi is in the car, ready to go.'

Zac's mind was doing calculations at a rapid pace and coming up with nothing useful. How did he…?

He saw Tom look past him down the hall. 'Evie, you're coming, too. Excellent.' He winked at Zac and almost certainly would have thumped him on the back if Evie hadn't been right there.

'Where?'

'The Big Night Out. We're sitting outside in deference to our advanced ages but it'll be fun. We don't get much live entertainment down this way. Get your gear, let's go.'

'I promised I'd go with old Mr Louis, but he hasn't called.' Her face was open and happy and, except for lips that were slightly pink and swollen, there was no clue as to what had just happened. Would Tom work it out? If he did, Zac would get no peace. 'I think he was just toying with my affections,' Evie was saying about Mr Louis.

Tom hooted with laughter and five minutes later they were all in Lexi's car—she'd given him a most unsubtle wink when she'd spotted Evie—heading for the concert.

Which was one way, reflected Zac an hour later, to get his date with her. Tom and Lexi had left to wander around the perimeter of the concert, leaving him to try and work out what had happened between him and Evie, but there was no point in talking about it—the music was pounding in their ears.

The concert was being staged near the foreshore on a grassy square bounded on two sides by two of the oldest, and most popular, hotels in town. The other sides faced the sea, separated from the beach by a strip of park. They were now sitting in the park near the town's Ferris wheel.

Kids wandered in and out of the gates in the temporary fencing delineating the concert from the public areas. Were they looking for things—drugs?—they couldn't access inside or just being kids with short attention spans? For once Zac decided to let it go—tonight it wasn't his concern. There was an increased police presence, he'd noticed several teams of police with sniffer

dogs patrolling the streets and plenty of ambu-
lances about, too, including trained paramedics
from Adelaide, so tonight he could relax.

One young couple sat on a bench nearby, the
boy pulling the girl onto his lap where they kissed
hungrily, his hand snaking inside her T-shirt. The
noise of the band carried across to them, the
slight ocean breeze not strong enough to whisk
the music away.

'I'm too old for this,' he mouthed at Evie above
the scream of base guitars and screeching
vocals—was that singing? It made Evie's voice
sound like an opera singer's.

'I *knew* I should've come with Mr Louis,' she
mouthed back, her eyes alight with mischief—
and happiness?

If she was feeling uncertain after their kiss, she
didn't show it. She hadn't missed a beat, chatting
naturally in the car on the way here and once
they'd arrived until the roar of the music had
made conversation impossible.

Whereas he was filled with mixed emotions,
with questions, and few, if any, answers. He stiff-
ened momentarily as she leant further into his
side, resting her head against his chest in such a
way he had to wrap his arm about her shoulders

to support her there. It shouldn't feel so natural, so good, if it was wrong. But he knew she *was* wrong for him. Or he was wrong for her? Or maybe the issue was precisely that she *felt* right for him.

He thought of the reasons he didn't date. The one, non-negotiable reason. A reason not even a gorgeous belly-dancing woman with a terrible singing voice, a warm sense of humour and a wonderful natural touch with children could persuade him from.

Not even if she kissed like a passionate gypsy.

She looked up at him as if she'd sensed the direction of his thoughts, and a tiny, teasing smile played around her lips. Over the jarring sound of the music he couldn't be sure if she'd whispered the request or he'd just imagined it but, either way, he knew he'd been lying to himself. Evie was challenging his resolve and she was winning.

Couldn't he have just one night?

Reason be damned, he thought, suddenly angry he'd been forced to make a choice.

One night with Evie? One night kissing this incredible woman who'd be gone soon? Was it too much to ask?

He looked deep into her eyes, his desire mirrored there by her own. That was his undoing.

He bent his head over hers and kissed her, all sensible, reasonable, rational thoughts obliterated by the all-consuming idea of Evie.

He was kissing her in public, in the middle of town. She'd never have thought he'd do that. But there was no way she was going to stop him so she put her heart and soul into kissing him back, the sound of the concert receding into the background as she focussed on Zac.

A wolf-whistle distracted her. She opened one eye a smidgen. If the whistles were for them she'd be getting no more kisses in public. She broke away, felt his body tense as he, too, opened his eyes and glanced around. But the attention was focussed elsewhere.

Two young girls traipsed by, their long legs and perfect figures on display. In very short skirts and minuscule tops, they tottered on three-inch heels, followed closely by a few teenage boys. They looked like the college kids she remembered from her schooldays, the boys all dressed in the 'uniform' of expensive, branded board shorts and surf T-shirts with slip-on leather thongs or unlaced trainers on their feet. They held beer bottles and from the snatches of conversation Evie could hear, it sounded as though they'd had a few drinks already.

There was another whistle, followed by a suggestive comment, and both had come from a couple of boys—locals?—who were approaching from the opposite direction. Evie saw the girls hesitate, slowing their steps to let their male companions catch up. Safety in numbers?

Evie felt Zac sit up a little straighter, watching carefully, one arm still around her shoulders. The band had finished its set and there was relative quiet now. She sensed trouble.

The boys with the attitude had stopped on the path, about twenty metres from where she and Zac sat, blocking the girls' path. The girls stepped onto the grass but the boys moved across, blocking them again, making obscene gestures, laughing loudly.

Two of the college boys looked around nervously but the third, taller and bigger than the rest, kept walking, stopping an inch away from the others, shielding the girls with his body.

'Give it up, guys, they're with us.' Their voices were clearly audible over the background noise of the crowd.

'You don't know what you're missing, girls,' said one of the locals, leaving no doubt as to his meaning and accompanying his words with explicit gestures.

'In your dreams,' retorted one of the girls.

Keep quiet! Evie thought.

Zac and Evie stood at the same time, both sensing this could go either way.

'You won't have time to dream if you come with us.'

'I said, leave it.' The bigger college kid wasn't backing down.

'You gonna make us?' The kid pushed past, deliberately bumping into the college boy, shoulder to shoulder. As he went past, the college kid stuck a foot out, tripping his antagonist and sending him sprawling across the footpath.

His mate shoved the college kid backwards and Zac started moving, but the first punch had been thrown. The college boy had tossed his beer bottle away, shattering it on the ground, and he'd got the first proper punch in. The local kid who had tripped got to his feet and that seemed to mobilise the other two boys, who'd been trying to blend into the background. It was three against two, but the college boys didn't look as if they'd had much experience in street fighting. One was felled by a punch in the face and went down in a crumpled heap, blood pouring from his nose. The other was shoved and sent staggering backwards, colliding with the girls.

In slow motion, Evie watched as one girl went flying, landing heavily on the edge of the footpath. She sat up, screaming, looking at her hand. Evie could see the broken neck of the beer bottle embedded in the girl's palm and raced to assist, barely registering that Zac was now in the middle of the fight. It was two against two now but the fight would have to wait.

'Zac. I need help,' she yelled at him, as she ran towards the girl.

She saw Zac turn his head in her direction, distracted by her voice. Too late she realised what she'd done. She stopped dead and tried to yell a warning as she saw the kid take aim, but her voice deserted her. Zac was looking directly at her and must have seen something in her expression because he ducked, but not fast enough. The kid's fist hit him beside his eye, splitting the skin.

Zac was bleeding. He wouldn't thank her for that, but she couldn't afford to worry about him now. 'Stop it. All of you. I need help,' she shouted, and this time she got everyone's attention. She crouched beside the girl, who was still screaming, and saw Zac had turned his back on the fight and was heading her way. Fortunately his departure seemed to defuse the situation and the boys gave up the fight. The two local boys strutted off, still swearing, but at least they were going.

The girl had pulled the broken glass out of her hand and was squeezing her palm closed with her other hand, trying to stop the blood flow.

'I'm Evie, I'm a nurse. What's your name?'

'Sally,' the girl said between sobs, her face pale.

The other kids had crowded around, forcing Zac to push through them to reach Evie. He squatted beside her and she motioned to him. 'Zac is a doctor.' The kids gave him incredulous looks—not surprising really, he was a mess. He looked more like a shaggy bear than ever now, his hair was sticking out all over his head, his face smeared with blood, his own probably, as the cut above his eye continued to bleed.

Sally was shivering, despite the warmth of the night. One of the boys had a lightweight cotton jumper tied around his waist.

'I need your top to keep her warm, she's in

shock.' He handed it over and Evie wrapped it around Sally's shoulders as she told Zac what had happened.

'Can I have a look at your hand?' Zac asked. He prised her fingers away, opening up her palm. Blood covered everything, making it difficult in the darkness to see exactly what damage had been done. 'Does anyone have any water?'

The other girl passed Zac her water bottle. He stripped off his shirt, turning it inside out, and then took the bottle and removed the lid. He poured water over the injured girl's hand, holding it at an angle so the water ran off, washing the blood away. Evie tore her gaze away from Zac's naked torso as an image of a gladiator, bloodied and bruised from battle, replaced that of a shaggy bear. She could see the gash at the base of Sally's thumb and forced herself to concentrate on that. It was still bleeding but fortunately the glass had sliced into a vein, not an artery, and the blood flow was relatively slow.

'We'll have to wait until we get you to the hospital to have a proper look at your hand. It needs stitching at the least, and I can't do that here.' Zac tore his T-shirt into strips, packing some against the wound, tying it in place with more strips of fabric.

As he worked, he spoke to Evie. 'Can you call Tom? We need a lift.'

She was about to ask for the number when she saw Tom and Lexi hurrying towards them.

'What's going on?'

'Long story, but we need a lift to the hospital.' Zac was wiping blood from his brow as he spoke. Too late, Evie remembered her scarf tied around her hips. Undoing this, she pressed it to Zac's forehead in an attempt to stem the blood flow. Zac put his hand to his eye, placing it over Evie's hand, his palm warm on her cool skin.

Tom didn't waste time with more questions. 'I'll get the car.'

'Lexi, do you mind waiting here? I'd like Evie to come with us and Sally's friend.' Zac indicated the other girl with a tilt of his head. 'I'll send Tom straight back.'

'Of course. Do you want me to get the police?'

Zac shook his head. 'I can't imagine anyone will want to make a complaint. They're all at fault and this injury was just an accident.'

Tom pulled up at the kerb and Evie and Zac bundled Sally and the other girl, Zoe, into the car. Zac turned back to the boys who were standing, dumbstruck, on the footpath beside Lexi. 'Lexi's a doctor, too. Wait here with her and Tom'll come back and drop you home.' The boys nodded, looking completely bewildered.

Tom pulled into the ambulance bay and Zac and Evie ushered the girls into the emergency department. Libby was on duty and she didn't know where to look as they walked through the doors, Zac shirtless and covered in blood, one eye hidden behind a scrap of fabric, with two teenage girls in tow.

Zac grabbed a clean gown from a trolley, throwing it on backwards, like a shirt, restoring some semblance of modesty. Evie directed Sally and Zoe to an examination cubicle before starting to fill Libby in on the situation. She sat Sally in a chair as Libby wheeled a table into place, positioning Sally's hand on the tabletop before fetching two blankets from the warming cupboard, one for each of the girls.

Evie went to wash her hands and, standing beside Zac as he wiped his hands dry, she was treated to a display of rippling chest muscles under his open gown. He had the body of an athlete and she wondered what exercise he did. She had a serious case of lust going on here. She knew so little about him but she knew she wanted more.

Libby settled next to Zac, anticipating his needs as she administered analgesia and swabbed the blood away. Evie was left to play the role of spectator, left to watch Zac.

'You've cut a vein and damaged a tendon, possibly a nerve as well. Injuries to a hand aren't something to take lightly. You need microsurgery and you'll need to be transferred to Adelaide tonight. I'll organise an ambulance but I need to speak to your parents. I assume they're your next of kin?'

Evie waited with Sally while Zac called her parents and made arrangements for an ambulance transfer. Once Sally was on her way, Evie took charge.

'Your turn,' she said to Zac.

'What for?'

'First aid. The cut on your head needs attention.'

Zac touched his fingers to his eyebrow then pulled them away to inspect them. 'It's stopped bleeding.'

Evie pushed him into a chair, not an easy task but he didn't resist her, and positioned an instrument trolley behind him as she answered. 'Only just. It still needs cleaning and a couple of steri-strips. Unless, of course, you'd prefer a scar?' It would probably suit him, add an air of mystery to his features, but it would be at odds with his reputation of being responsible and in control.

'Scars are only interesting if there's an interesting story behind them.'

'In that case, sit still and let me do my job.' She dragged a stool closer to Zac's chair and sat down, her thighs either side of his left knee. She had to be close in order to see what she was doing but the proximity was distracting. His chest, bare under the open gown, had a smattering of dark hair, leading her eyes lower. With an effort she kept her gaze directed at his forehead, avoiding his eyes, which she could feel were focussed on her. Pulling on surgical gloves over her clean hands, she swabbed Zac's wound with Betadine. He flinched at the sting but said nothing. She was sitting a fraction higher than him and each time he exhaled she could feel his warm breath brush over the base of her throat, filling the dip between her collar-bones. The sensation sent a tingle through her body, making it difficult to concentrate. If she left him with a scar, he'd only have himself to blame.

Evie removed three steri-strips and placed them carefully over the cut, pulling the edges together. 'All done.'

She dropped her gaze, finally meeting his eyes. He was still watching her, his gaze so intense it made her catch her breath. He was so confident in his skin, in his masculinity. Flustered, she dropped her gaze even further, down to his bare chest, but that didn't help. Not a bit.

'Thank you.' His voice was deep and rich and resonated through her body.

'My pleasure.'

Zac stood, affording her another eyeful of his broad chest. She felt herself flush and scooted backwards on the stool, out of arm's reach, before she was tempted to stretch a hand out to touch him.

'I'd better go. I need to see about getting Zoe home. Not quite the end I had in mind to the evening.'

'It's OK. I'm beat, I just want to fall into bed.'

Zac's grin matched the mischievous glint in his eyes, but he kept quiet, still in control. The interruption to their evening had broken their connection and Evie wasn't sure what would happen next. Maybe he'd taken tonight in his stride?

Relax, let it happen? Somehow she doubted it. It didn't fit his serious persona, but neither did oh, so delectable kisses under a golden moon.

He took her hand, rubbing his thumb in tiny circles over the tender skin of her wrist. 'I'd better go,' he repeated. 'We never did get that coffee. Can I take a rain-check?'

Evie nodded and watched him leave, with Zoe in tow, and wondered what tomorrow would bring.

'So we kissed. Big deal.' Evie was sitting on Letitia's bed, waiting for Jake and the girls to arrive. The retrieval team would be on their way to transfer Letitia to Adelaide and Evie had timed her lunch-break to coincide with it. 'We're both adults, why get all het up about it?' She kept her voice low since, as Letitia's doctor, Zac, would soon be there, too. She wasn't going to get caught out a second time, discussing him with her sister-in-law.

'Was it?' Letitia was in the spirit of things, despite her increasing nerves about leaving her family. Which was why Evie had introduced the topic, but now, having done so, she found she did need to talk about it for her own sake.

'Was it what?'

'A big deal?'

Evie closed her eyes and remembered, opening them again as Letitia started laughing. 'You don't need to answer that, your expression said it all.'

'What did it say?'

'It was a *very* big deal.'

Evie grinned. 'I didn't say it wasn't heart-stoppingly great, just there's no need to get het up about it.'

'I suspect he is.'

'He is what?'

'Getting het up.'

'Why?'

'He's been a dedicated bachelor ever since he arrived here and, as far as I know, he doesn't date so my guess is he'll be thinking this over.'

'Great,' Evie moaned. 'He'll probably decide he's made a big mistake and head for the hills.'

'Now who's getting het up? It was just a kiss, you said.'

Letitia was laughing and Evie knew it was at her expense. Zac's kisses had been amazing. They couldn't mean nothing! 'Maybe I need to ask Fel. I need some inside information.'

'Zac's Aunt Fel?'

'Yes. I've met her. She said you're one of her favourite staff members and I've seen for myself how much she adores the girls.'

At the mention of her girls, tears threatened to well up in Letitia's eyes. Oops, time for some more distraction. 'Have you got some good books to take with you?'

'You know I'm not much of a reader, not like you.'

'It's never too late. I wasn't always a voracious reader but when you're totally out of it for three years, like I was, you kind of have no choice.'

The door opened, admitting Zac, as Evie was speaking.

'Totally out of what?' Zac asked, his tone cautious.

Evie and Letitia both ignored his question as they stared openly at his face. The cut across his eyebrow was almost unnoticeable as it was overshadowed by the discolouration around the eye itself. His eye was purple and swollen and half-closed.

Letitia was full of sympathy. 'You look dreadful. Does it hurt?'

Zac touched it self-consciously and then grimaced. 'It's not too bad as long as I don't touch it.'

'Let me guess,' said Evie. 'We should see the other guy, right?'

'I have no idea how he looks—he ran away.' Zac matched her quip but there was a reservation in his voice that hadn't been there last night. Was that just because they weren't alone? Or was there something more? She'd thought he might pull away but hadn't thought it would be so quickly.

'I never picked you for a tough guy,' said Letitia.

'I'm not. I'm tipping the other bloke looks fine, I didn't lay a finger on him,' Zac answered Letitia but was watching Evie, and she cursed silently as she felt herself blush. She turned away, wondering how she was going to explain this, but was saved from further embarrassment when laughter from outside the room announced the arrival of Jake, Mack and Gracie.

Letitia had insisted the girls not see her leave in the ambulance or even being put on the gurney, and the girls had insisted they say goodbye. A compromise had been struck that the transfer team would take Letitia downstairs in a wheelchair and Mack and Gracie would say their goodbyes on the ward.

The transfer team, two young men, entered with the wheelchair, swelling the room past capacity but Evie knew the distractions would help Letitia cope.

She sneaked a glance at Zac. What was it about him that had so quickly made her forget her plan to befriend him, to help him lighten up? Those intentions had been overtaken by one thought only—to be kissed much, much more by him.

Unlike Evie, Letitia only had eyes for the wheelchair.

A riot of colours, it was decorated in a combination of paper streamers and hand-made cards bearing crayon-scrawled messages of 'Get well soon, Mummy, love Mack' and 'I lov yoo, Mummy, love Gracie.' A few pink balloons drifted behind for good measure. It was so heavily decorated the wheelchair itself was scarcely visible.

Letitia blinked back tears and held her arms open for her daughters, who scrambled up next to her on the bed. 'That's the most beautiful sight in the world.' She dropped a kiss on each little head and Evie knew she was talking about her girls, one cradled in each arm, not the wheelchair.

'We're going to come to see you after the operation.' Gracie's eyes were open wide, bright with excitement, oblivious to the real situation.

'And…' She dropped her voice to a loud whisper. 'We're getting a *day off school!*'

Her comment lifted general spirits for the goodbyes and Letitia managed to keep her tears at bay, at least until the lift doors had closed on the group which included Zac and Jake. Evie doubted the bravery would last much beyond the lift ride. She squatted down and scooped a niece to each side of her, kissing the tops of their heads just as their mother had done.

But the image that stayed with her was of Zac's face as the lift doors had closed. He'd kept his gaze on her. Even when she'd broken it to look at Letitia and Jake, she'd felt it. And if there'd been questions in his eyes before, there'd at least been desire. But now? For some reason, only the questions were there.

There was something else about Evie, something other than her ability to get under his defences, something that had been niggling at his peace of mind since he'd first seen her.

It's never too late, she'd been saying to Letitia as he'd entered the room. *When you're totally out of it for three years, like I was, you kind of have no choice.*

She'd known exactly what they'd been dealing with when Stewart had been brought in. Not just that it had been drugs, but which drug. She'd been spot on.

Was that why she'd been 'out of it' for three years?

When?

And if she had been, what did it matter to him as long as she was no longer using and not a risk to their patients? She couldn't be into drugs if she was as good at her job as she seemed, could she? He could ask her—but would she admit she'd had a problem? And if she didn't have a history, he'd risk offending her. No, no risk, it was a certainty.

But he didn't know her at all. All he knew was she was capable of dismissing all reasonable, rational thought from his mind. He'd kissed her, damn it, on two occasions last night. He hadn't known he'd been going to do it and he never did something he hadn't planned, debated or come to a sensible decision about.

She was unlike anyone he'd ever met. He was a planner and she made him forget about plans. So, chequered past or not, she was dangerous.

The problem was, it felt good to forget.

He was in danger of wanting more.

But more of Evie meant he'd be less in control.

And there were great big questions hanging over her head. Questions he needed answered, not just for his sake but for the sake of the hospital.

Their little group was moving at a great pace through the hospital and he focussed on the couple in front of him. He needed answers, he couldn't think rationally without information. Could he ask Letitia? Jake?

What else had Evie said when they'd met with Stewart's parents? She'd agreed with Stewart's dad that if Stewart used drugs they'd be unlikely to know. Did she know that because she'd managed to keep *her* past—her present—a secret?

They reached the ambulance bay, the warmth of a summer's day easing over his skin, but he was scarcely aware of it. Letitia was saying goodbye to Jake, who'd follow the next morning to be with her in time for the surgery. Tears were running freely down her face. Jake was still being strong but he was holding his wife tight, like he didn't want to let go.

So, no, now was not the time to poke around in Evie's past.

'Thanks for everything, Zac, you've been wonderful.' Jake had released Letitia from the hug and she was wiping tears from her cheeks with one hand, holding Jake's hand with her other.

'No thanks necessary,' he said, and he meant it. 'You just concentrate on getting better and coming back to us as soon as you can. I'll come to see you after the op.'

'You don't need to do that. I know how busy you are.'

'Consider it part of the after-sales service.' Letitia managed a smile at that. 'And strictly no worrying about your girls, we'll all be looking out for them. And they've got Evie. They're in good hands.'

But as he watched Letitia being lifted into the ambulance and stood aside as husband and wife held eye contact until the doors closed, saw the trust and love between them, simple, strong and plain, he repeated his last phrase to himself.

They're in good hands.

But were they?

Jake had excused himself quickly to return to his daughters, eager to spend time with them before he left for Adelaide, leaving Zac free to do what he'd intended when he'd first met Evie: check her personnel file. He'd meant to do it but had been sidetracked. Correction, had allowed himself to be sidetracked, had convinced himself he didn't need to know more. But he did.

One benefit of being responsible for sorting out personnel problems was that he didn't have to voice his concerns to a third party to get her file checked, he could do it himself, discreetly. Not that the file would tell him much—she'd have been unlikely to declare a drug-use history in a job application form.

Unlocking the personnel manager's office door, he scanned the filing cabinets. Locating the G–O drawer, it took only a second to find her file and retrieve it, trying to ignore the feeling he was snooping. He wasn't, he had a legitimate concern and he'd be negligent not to look into it. He'd do the same for anyone else. *But she's not anyone else,* was the whisper in his ear as he read and reread the large print of the label on the cover: Ms Eva Henderson.

If he found out she had such a past, what then? What steps would he have to take?

He stood with the file in his hand for thirty seconds before he could open it, and when he did, he flipped it open like it could bite.

Her personal history was summarised on the first page. The plain black and white page seemed at odds with the vibrant woman who'd already got under his skin. Born, raised and schooled in rural New South Wales. Gained her nursing qualifications in the UK. He knew the school, it had a good reputation. Nothing much there. Flipping over pages with impatience, he reached the references. The first was from a consultant no less. In what universe did consultants write references for nursing staff? *Ms Henderson would be an asset in any hospital.* And another, from her locum agency by the look of it. *We wish Ms Henderson all the best for her return to Australia. She leaves knowing she has a place with us at any time in the future should she choose.*

There were more. He skimmed them, knowing they wouldn't tell him what he needed to know, but they were telling him what he wanted to know—Evie was a great nurse, highly skilled, well regarded, reliable, empathic. The list of adjectives went on.

He flipped back to her employment history. She'd started with a permanent job at St Martin's in London and had resigned less than six months later. Since then she'd been solely employed in casual work. Why? There was one main reason he could think of for a new graduate to quit a secure job in a prestigious hospital—the pay was better doing contract work. Which was no crime. Lord knew, nurses were generally grossly underpaid considering their responsibilities and training. But had she had a particular reason for needing more money? An expensive habit to support?

Glancing back up the page, the dates listed next to each entry came into sharper focus. Each year, for the past five years, there was a gap of three or four months her dates of employment didn't cover. Those months simply weren't listed.

He looked up, the file gripped in one hand, glanced at his watch and cursed. He was running late. The missing months would have to wait.

But he knew already she hadn't spent that time in Australia. Letitia had made it clear how excited they had all been to see her, saying Evie had only had a few flying visits home to see the girls, as she couldn't afford any more time off work. What excuse had she made to her family when she'd had so much time away from work but hadn't been able to make time for them?

More to the point, where *had* she been and what had she been doing?

The missing months were only part of it. If he'd overheard right, there were three other *years* to be accounted for.

He cursed. Why, when he hadn't kissed a woman since his marriage had disintegrated, did his resolve have to be so tested now?

Evie was addictive and he wanted more; despite his doubts and all the reasons not to, he wanted more.

More of her time, more of her laughter, more of her kisses.

But that path was closed to him. That was non-negotiable. He'd learnt that lesson with his ex-wife—it was the legacy he had to live with.

But there were moments of madness when Evie made him forget about his past and the constraints on his future.

How was that possible when in over three years he hadn't lost sight of his resolutions even once?

Just who was Evie Henderson?

CHAPTER FIVE

JUST who was this man who could kiss her like he'd never stop, then go cold in an instant? He'd gone cold while she'd still been bubbling away at boiling point at the mere thought of how she'd felt in his arms…

Her thoughts took their own course as she made her way to the nursing-home. Her shift was almost over but she'd been called to assist with a resident who'd fallen. She was on an early and after today she'd need to race to get the girls from school. Today her brother was still at home, so it didn't matter if she went over time but tomorrow he was leaving—and then what? How was she going to juggle everything without the huge inconvenience that had just sideswiped her? She was falling for Zac.

Damn and double damn, she didn't need that. Having family ties here made it hard enough to stay away for such long periods of time. Another temptation to sway her from her chosen path was not what she was looking for. She was already torn constantly between her two lives, always feeling guilty about not doing enough in one camp or the other.

Striding rapidly to the nursing-home, she saw Zac in the distance, eyes cast down, walking with a file gripped in his hand, his steps swift as if he was late for something. Her heart all but stopped in her chest at the sight of him, at the memory of him kissing her. And how!

Her reaction confirmed it: she was falling for him. She couldn't argue with that conclusion when a quick glimpse of him was all it took to leave her feeling as though she'd been physically knocked off her feet.

'What's up, love?' Mr Louis was sitting in the warmth of the afternoon sunshine, and his question broke into her reverie.

'Mr Louis! Hello. Sorry I can't stop, someone's had a fall.' She hoped he hadn't seen her leap as he'd spoken, so deep had she been in her thoughts.

'Probably Wilf doing acrobatics again, old fool, just won't accept his youth is over,' she heard him call out as she sped towards the entrance doors.

She entered the common room to find Pam crouched next to a prostrate figure. She was holding a pad firmly over a cut on the person's head, soaking up blood, and another beside the patient's mouth.

Fel?

The situation took her thoughts straight back to Zac. She glanced around. Zac hadn't been heading this way, he might not even know. The residents who'd gathered around stepped aside to make room for her and she knelt down beside Fel.

'What happened?'

'Fel had a fall. Her knee is playing up and it went from under her. She hit her head on the side of the table.' Pam nodded at a wooden table, its edges sharp. 'She also bit her lip, she's given herself a nasty cut with her teeth. I haven't tried to move her, just in case.' Evie nodded. 'The orderlies are on their way, they were all busy in Theatre.'

'Hold the pads down as much as you can while I check her over. We really need clean cold water on her lip, but I'll check her first.'

Evie started her examination, moving her hands gently over the old lady who had rapidly become one of her three favourite residents—Fel, Nancy and Mr Louis. She explained what she was doing to both Pam and Fel as she worked, but Fel, though conscious, wasn't answering.

The bleeding from her lip and the cut on her forehead was subsiding. 'You'll have a nasty headache and perhaps some stitches to show for this afternoon, Fel, but it looks as though you're OK otherwise. I'm sure the doctor will want a CT scan and you might be kept in hospital overnight for observation. Other than that, your knee will need looking into if you're not already seeing someone for it.'

'She's a stubborn old girl.'

At the sound of Zac's voice behind her, Evie started to get up but overbalanced, collecting Zac with the full force of her movement as she stumbled into his chest. Too close, too intimate. Was she flushed? Touching a hand to her cheek, she kept her face turned from him, bending back down to Fel.

It didn't help. He crouched down, too, and the proximity was disconcerting. Not that he seemed affected. His concentration was solely on Fel and he scarcely seemed to notice Evie was there. So one of them was in control of their emotions and, no surprises, it was him.

'You didn't need to come over,' mumbled Fel.

'I told them not to bother you, Tom will come and see me.'

'Tom won't be at the hospital for a good few hours so you get what you get, and that's me.'

The orderlies arrived and the room felt crowded. Evie felt superfluous but didn't know if she should go or stay with Fel.

Zac stood, addressing the orderlies. 'Take her to Radiology, please.' To his aunt, he said, 'I'll go ahead and get a CAT scan organised. I'm not expecting to find anything, but with a knock and a cut like that, it needs to be done. Either way, you'll stay in hospital overnight.'

He nodded at Pam and Evie and left, leaving the orderlies to transfer Fel to a stretcher and Evie to trail along with them to Radiology, confused. He wouldn't want to make it obvious he'd kissed her, wouldn't want to single her out for any special attention, but he'd scarcely made eye contact with her.

What had happened since he'd kissed her? What had changed? Or was it nothing to do with her? A bad day at work, perhaps?

The trouble was, she didn't know him well enough to guess. His kisses melted her soul, he was a fantastic cook and he seemed like a brilliant doctor—but what else did she really know about him? According to his great-aunt, he'd had a nasty relationship breakdown but what red-blooded man decided to ignore a physical attraction like theirs? Not one she'd ever known.

She refused to be ignored—she'd make him talk. But when? She'd promised to take the girls to the beach after work and Jake would be at home tonight, but from tomorrow she'd be on her own with her nieces. That would make it hard to catch Zac, especially if he didn't want to be caught. She left Fel in the care of the radiographers and went off duty, mulling over her options.

He'd catch Evie tonight, Zac decided as he slid his aunt's scan up on the light box. The radiologist had given Fel the all-clear but he wanted to see for himself. He'd make sure Fel was comfortable. And then he'd do his sleuthing. His bridge-burning.

He should be calling Evie into his office, quizzing her at work, but he'd kissed her—so how could he do that? One kiss then—bam! The next day he was forced into investigating her background, tossing up whether to accuse her of using or having used drugs. Not the best way to follow up their first date—not that he'd call it that. Tom and Lexi and fate had orchestrated it. He didn't date.

As it was, Fel was asleep so there went the first item on his list. He'd have to come back and see her later, after dinner, which meant trawling through Evie's file and then, if that didn't clear up his questions, confronting her jumped up a notch. He wasn't ready!

Tucking her file under his arm, he left the hospital and headed home, the summer light still strong. When had he last left work at this time, even though it was late enough for dinner? But staying at his desk to tackle paperwork or search for answers to the funding crisis wasn't where he wanted to be right now.

Neither was doubting Evie.

Which meant he spent the next half-hour chopping, mixing and stir-frying, creating a delicious dinner a full two hours earlier than he'd normally eat but not able to create a solution to the Evie problem. The file remained where he'd dropped it on the kitchen bench.

His meal finished and cleared away, he headed back to his bedroom to grab a T-shirt, having donned only faded old jeans when he'd arrived home. A knock at the front door waylaid him.

Evie. Her hair was wet, pulled back into a mess of a ponytail, and she smelt like the ocean. A light summer dress floated around her.

'Can I come in?'

She stepped inside, not waiting for an answer—or did he nod? She headed for the kitchen, Zac adding a belated 'Sure' as he followed her along the passage.

This meeting was premature—he had nothing to say to her yet, he hadn't finished looking at the file. But he couldn't pretend he had no issues either. Which left him—where, exactly?

Which left him playing host. 'Can I get you a drink?'

'Thanks. We've been at the beach and I've played one too many games of stuck-in-the-mud and jumped one too many waves.'

'The girls had fun?' He was at a loss for something to say but he cringed inwardly as he came out with the obvious.

She nodded and perched on a bar stool, watching him as he grabbed glasses and filled them with cold water from the fridge. Why did she have to look so at home there? So right? He'd have to come out with his questions soon or it would become impossible if he played the polite host for too long. Deep breath. Just ask about the missing months.

'Why have you got my file?'

Damn, he'd left it out in full-view, her name in bold letters across the front. The role of polite host evaporated as he tried and discarded various answers to distract her from her question.

'Are you checking up on me?' She'd got it straight away, but she didn't seem angry. 'Have I done something wrong?' She seemed worried. Was that good or bad?

'Not exactly.' Not yet. 'But you said something today that I needed to check. And I didn't have a chance at work so I brought your file home. You weren't meant to see it.'

'And now that I have? What is it you need to check?'

He glanced at the file.

'You can ask me directly if you like.' She was too distracting, perched on his stool, the worry on her face replaced by something approaching amusement—at his obvious discomfort, no doubt. 'I'm right here.'

'You are, indeed.'

'Ah. And you don't want me to be. It must be pretty bad, whatever it is you think I've done.'

She sounded chatty. Who made small talk in a situation like this? Apparently she did.

'I haven't finished looking. I don't want to ask you questions that could offend you when I haven't finished reading your file. I'm sure it'll clear it up.'

'I promise not to be offended. Come on, out with it, it'll save you time.' Head tilted to one side, she teased him with a tiny smile. 'You know you want to.'

She was too, too distracting.

He focussed, with difficulty. 'Have you ever used drugs?'

'Never. Next question?'

'You're not on drugs now?'

'I think that's covered in my first answer, but you're new at this, I can tell, so I'll humour you. No, I am one hundred per cent not on drugs now.' She drew a finger across her chest in the shape of a cross. 'Haven't even had a Panadol for weeks and weeks, and I'm happy to swear to that. Next?'

'You're taking this awfully well, if what I'm asking you is totally off base.'

'Zac, you're on the board of the hospital, I need my job, I don't think abusing you is the right response. Besides,' she added cheerfully, 'abusing people is not my style. Why drugs, just out of interest? It's not to do with Stewart, is it, or you would've asked me this earlier?'

If he didn't sit down, he'd fall down. He sat on the stool opposite her. 'You said to Letitia today you were out of it for three years.' By the twinkle in her eye, there was a joke he wasn't in on. 'And your file says you have three or four months off work every year.'

'And you think I'm off perfecting my drug-taking techniques or maybe it's harvest time and I'm farming my drug crop?'

'If I'm on the wrong track, you'll think I'm crazy, but I have to know for sure. It's—'

'Your responsibility, I know. And I'd hate to be the one to come between you and responsibility. Not when you're so good at it.' She caught the look on his face and laughed. 'Sorry, I imagine these sorts of investigations come with a strictly no-teasing-allowed tag. You'll have to forgive me, I haven't been investigated as a potential drug lord before. I'm not au fait with the procedure.'

'Evie,' he said, 'awkward or not, I'd appreciate an explanation.'

'I hate to disabuse you of the notion that I'm

an underworld figure, it sounds so much more dramatic and alluring than the truth. Are you sure we can't leave it like that?'

'Quite sure.'

She pulled a face at him and hitched up her dress to rub the back of one slender, beautifully formed knee. 'Drat the mossies,' she said. 'I miss my Australian summers terribly, except for the mosquitoes. They love me, eat me alive, even on the beach. I'd put spray on, except—' she was suppressing a laugh '—I hate using the stuff, all sorts of awful toxins in them.'

'Evie.'

'Oh, all right, it was worth a try. Reason why I'm not on drugs, number one. Or rather, reason why I was out of it for three years, they're interchangeable, I imagine. I had chronic fatigue syndrome during high school and missed most of years nine through to eleven. I made it back for my final year but I was pretty behind by then, so the marks I'd always taken for granted I'd get didn't come my way.'

'Chronic fatigue syndrome?'

She screwed up her perfect nose. 'See? Not nearly as mysterious and enticing as you were thinking.'

'I'd hardly use those words to describe being a drug user.'

'You're right, of course. I just hate having to think about being sick. I made a promise to myself years ago not to think about it, just to make sure it never happened again. Which is also why I'd be the last person, ever, to use drugs. I don't even touch alcohol. Apart from being boringly dedicated to the pursuit of good health...' she raised a finger, as if considering something '...with the exception of my daily dose of coffee, there is no way I'm befuddling my senses with substances other than natural ones. I've missed out on three years, I'm not missing any more.'

It sounded feasible. It also fitted with the fact she was a glowing picture of good health. But...

'The months off work? Let me guess, a hard-core health farm?'

'Now you're teasing, which isn't professional of you.' She hesitated and he sensed she was stalling for time—didn't she want to tell him?

'You're drug-free but you're an ex-con on the run? Some secret life no one knows about?'

She was fidgeting with the hem of her dress, showing him those legs again. As a distraction technique, it was fantastic. He could hardly remember what he'd just asked her.

'Nothing secret and nothing illegal, just a bit unusual. There's no reason you shouldn't know,' she added, seemingly more to herself than to him. 'It's there somewhere in my file anyway. Those "missing months", as you call them, I spend in Vietnam.'

Vietnam. 'Why?' As she'd said, it probably was in her file, he just hadn't had time to find the details.

'I got involved with a foundation there, just as a volunteer, a number of years back. The foundation works with disadvantaged children and it's become so much a part of my life that I deliberately choose work that pays me well enough so I can indulge my wish to be involved.'

So he had the answer to why she'd quit a permanent, prestigious job soon after graduation. She'd wanted the money casual work offered but not for any reason he'd guessed.

'So there you have it, the complete summary of my life, work and interests, all in one neat package.'

'You don't look happy when you say that.'

'Only because the package isn't so neat at the moment. I was meant to be there now but I was needed here.' She shrugged a slender shoulder.

'Don't get me wrong, I wanted to come, Jake and Letitia didn't pressure me at all, but I still feel I'm letting everyone in Vietnam down.'

'What were you going to be doing that someone else couldn't do?'

'It's more a matter of whether there's anyone available to help. There are a lot of people committed to helping but there's never enough and if I'm not there, they're short one more. They're desperate for people with skills, especially in the health-care area.'

'You don't feel spending months there every year has been a decent enough contribution?'

'It's not just guilt—I feel an almost physical pull to be there. This is the first time in years I haven't been able to go and I'm feeling weird about it. Incomplete maybe. If that doesn't sound too pretentious.'

'Not pretentious, just saint-like.'

She laughed. 'I'm no saint. I'm talking about the personal satisfaction I get. So, really, it's all about me.' The sparkle in her eyes was back.

'What does the organisation do?'

'It was established to help street kids, children with no options, no homes, no future. It's expanded significantly to provide medical help in

a number of clinics, there's a school for disadvantaged children, including those with disabilities,
a vocational training programme. The list goes
on. There are all sorts of people all over the world
who make it possible, I only play a small part.'

'Your eyes light up when you talk about it. It
means a lot to you.'

'It means the world to me to be involved.' There
was the slightest pucker between her eyebrows,
the only indication she was mulling something
over. 'So this is why you were behaving strangely
today? You thought I had some deep, dark secret?
You *were* keeping your distance, weren't you?'

Her directness, her openness, her apparent
ability to let his suspicions wash over her cut
through his own natural instinct to keep his
feelings under wraps.

'I had some doubts. We have to work together.
Conflicts between work and personal life are
guaranteed. And when I overheard you talking
about missing three years, I panicked.'

'Didn't your mother tell you eavesdropping
never brings good news? But now you know I'm
squeaky clean, so there's no problem.'

Looking at her, swinging her legs as she sat on
his stool, hair dried now into a riot of dark curls,

she looked delicious. She looked like she belonged. But she didn't, she was passing through, this was a temporary—and maybe not entirely welcome—hiatus from her usual life.

He knew he'd been looking for excuses when he'd grabbed her file. Hoping to find something in there to help get her out of his head. But it hadn't worked. She'd done nothing wrong. Nothing except stir his libido.

But that was a no-go area. How could he stick to his resolve if she was there, forcing him to confront the fact there was a whole part of his life he couldn't share?

No problem, she'd said.

But he had big problems. And the biggest was that every time she swung her leg or flicked her hair over her shoulder or looked at him with her enormous brown eyes, it got more and more difficult to remember why he should stay away. Far away.

'Evie?'

'Yes?'

She'd never imagined, when she'd knocked on his door that night, that he'd be reaching for her like he was aching for her.

It was exactly what she wanted. And needed.

So there was no question of saying no, of reminding him he was saying one thing and doing another. That was his problem, not hers! She opened herself to his touch, sliding off the stool into his arms, moulding her body to the strong lines of his as she let herself melt into his kiss.

He tasted of the sea spray and salt she knew was on her own lips. Now it was his taste.

Her hands rested on his chest—the chest that had been distracting her from the moment he'd opened the door so she had no power against it now—fingers spread over the warmth of his skin, eyes closed, the world spinning slowly, so slowly it left only the two of them, with everything else ebbing away from her consciousness.

She could have stayed here for ever. In his arms, his lips on hers.

But she didn't have for ever.

And the time she had here was stolen time, stolen from a life she'd already committed to.

Casual flirtation was fine.

But what she was feeling now wasn't that. What she was feeling now was far from casual. What she was feeling now had 'danger' written all over it.

Danger? She should be running screaming in the opposite direction.

Instead, she leant in further and he deepened his kiss in response.

She had a crush—a schoolgirl crush. That's what it was. She'd missed out on so much in her adolescent years, it was only natural she'd regress at some point.

So she'd regress and enjoy it and take some memories with her when she left.

How long did crushes last?

CHAPTER SIX

CRUSHES were all very well but Evie had a sneaking suspicion hers was getting out of hand. She was working in Emergency, monitoring the oxygen sats on a teenager in the midst of a severe asthma attack, an easy job compared to some and one that left ample time for daydreaming. She'd never had fantasies about a dream wedding, not like some of her school friends. Her teenage fantasies had been about what she'd do when she got well—settling down had never crossed her mind, she was going to be a doctor or a lawyer or a physiotherapist. And then that hadn't worked out so, angry and disillusioned, she'd grabbed her backpack and fled overseas.

But if she'd had those dreams, it wasn't impossible to imagine Zac waiting for her at the end of the aisle. Thoughts of Zac had her skipping over the wedding and landing in the honeymoon, which was when she was interrupted by Libby.

'Evie, do you remember Stewart, the boy who was rushed in the other night?' Evie nodded. That sort of introduction to a job wouldn't slip her mind. 'He's here with his parents. They'd like a word if you have a minute.'

Evie handed over her monitoring to Libby and ducked out of the cubicle to find Stewart and his parents waiting for her.

'We didn't want to leave without saying thank you,' James said as he shook her hand enthusiastically.

'Glad to help.' She retrieved her hand and massaged her crushed fingers before turning her attention to Stewart. 'How are you feeling?'

He shrugged, maintaining a stubborn silence. Was he embarrassed? Dreading going home with his parents and being under what Evie knew would be his mother's vigilant monitoring? Or still feeling the effects of the ice?

'He's still tired, but you said to expect that.' Helen was filling in the awkward silence Stewart had created. 'I'll be glad to get home, that's for sure.'

'Did you see the news this morning?' James asked.

Evie shook her head.

'The police in Adelaide have arrested two men on drug charges. Pulled them over for traffic offences and found plastic containers of amphetamine paste, 20,000 hits worth. The police think they were heading for Pelican Beach.'

'I'm glad that's not going to make it to us.' Evie turned to Stewart, on the off chance he was receptive.

'Please, look after yourself, you only get one chance and that's particularly true where this drug is concerned.' Would he heed her warning? Who knew? She could only hope his parents would take what had happened seriously. Regardless, she'd done her job and now it was up to them as a family.

Her priority was to look after her own family and tomorrow she was taking the girls to visit Letitia. Zac was driving them and she let her mind drift back to her daydreaming as she returned to monitor her asthmatic patient.

If Evie had been dreaming of idyllic honeymoons while she'd worked, the drive to Adelaide put things into perspective. Gracie and Mack talked the whole way, leaving Evie no chance to talk to Zac, let alone daydream, and her powers of concentration were fading as they reached the hospital.

The lift doors opened, depositing their group onto the orthopaedic ward where they'd come to see Letitia. Evie scanned the corridor, looking for the nurses' station. Letitia was in Room Eight but Evie had no idea in which direction to head. Zac didn't hesitate and Evie and the girls fell in behind him.

Zac introduced himself to the ward clerk, who directed them to Letitia. The girls raced off, not concerned at all about the unfamiliar surroundings.

'Remember, girls, no jumping onto the bed, your mum will be sore,' Evie called after them.

'I want to speak to Letitia's surgeon if he's around the place,' Zac said to her. 'I'll join you in a moment.'

She met Mack and Grace at the door. 'In you go. Mum will be so excited to see you.' She pushed the door, holding it open as the girls sprinted in to their mother.

Letitia's smile lit up her face and she held her arms wide to embrace her daughters as they flung themselves at her, one on each side.

'Hello, my darlings,' she said, showering them with kisses. 'How are you?'

'Good. We brought you more pictures.' Gracie

and Mack allowed their dad to sneak a kiss in before they dug into their bags, pulling out their paintings. Sticking these to every available vertical surface around Letitia's bed served to keep them both occupied while Evie chatted with her brother and his wife.

'You look brighter than I expected.'

'I'm feeling good. The constant, deep pain in my hips has gone. My muscles are sore from the surgery and the exercises but I know those aches are only temporary.'

'You're even sitting out of bed.'

'This is fantastic.' Letitia indicated the armchair, its extendable legs raising it higher than a normal chair. 'I don't have to bend my hips too much to use it.'

'We'll need to hire one for home, I guess,' Jake said.

'And a few other things, but that's easy to organise, I'll sort it out with the rehab staff,' Evie replied.

'Thanks.'

'No problem. How long have you been sitting out for?'

'About ten minutes. I'm waiting for the physio to come to do my exercises with me.'

'Whose is this?' Gracie had found Letitia's walking frame and was swinging on it like a little monkey.

'That's mine.'

'It's like the ones in the nursing-home! Are you old now?'

Letitia laughed. 'Not very old, darling. I just need it while my muscles get strong.'

The door swung open, admitting Zac. Evie's heart leapt at the sight of him and her reaction surprised her. Twenty-eight years old and responding to a man like a hormone-riddled teenager? The smile Zac sent her way made her pulse race faster still as he crossed the room to shake Jake's hand and greet Letitia. 'I've just spoken to Mr Forrest. He seems very pleased with the surgery.'

'Now it's up to me to get through the rehab.' She grimaced.

'And to remember to take things slowly. You've got a long recovery ahead of you.'

'I know. I'm so relieved to have the surgery behind me, I'm not going to risk compromising the surgeon's efforts.'

'Glad to hear it. Evie's doing a great job with the girls, you've got nothing to worry about other than getting yourself better,' Zac said.

Letitia turned to her sister-in-law. 'Does that mean the girls have been getting some vegetables?'

'Not exactly, but I have remembered to take them to school and to make them lunches. That has to count for something.'

'It counts for a lot. I appreciate everything you're doing. You've put your life on hold for us.'

'I wouldn't have it any other way.'

'I'll do my best to make a quick recovery so you can return to your old life.'

'It will still be there whenever my services are no longer required here.'

Evie saw the questioning look Zac gave her but the arrival of the physio put paid to any further discussion.

'OK girls, why don't I take you to the zoo while Mum does her exercises?'

'Can we have an ice cream, Auntie Evie?'

'Gracie! Where are your manners?' Jake said.

'Can we have an ice-cream, *please?*'

'I meant, don't ask for treats!'

'It's OK,' Evie smiled. 'Yes, you can have an ice cream.'

'Are you coming too, Zac?'

'I'd love to, Mackenzie, but I have a meeting

in forty minutes,' he said as he glanced at his watch.

'That's OK, we can wait.' Mack sat down on Letitia's bed, her arms folded, and Jake chuckled at the sight of her.

'She looks just like you do, Evie, when you want something. She has that same stubborn expression.'

'Go, girl,' Evie said to Mack, high-fiving her. 'But we can't wait here because your mum needs to do her exercises and there's not enough room for all of us.'

'Please?' Mack was not giving up. Evie looked at Zac. Did he really want to go with them?

'I'll give you a call when my meeting is over and see if it's worth catching up with you.'

'Yippee!' said the girls. 'We'll see you later, Mum. Bye.' The girls kissed their parents and ran out of the room.

Evie followed and Zac caught her by the hand as they entered the corridor. 'If you walk through the botanical gardens, I'll wager you the girls will take at least half an hour following secret paths and whatnot. And then I shouldn't be too far behind you by the time you reach the zoo.'

'Sounds lovely.'

'It's signposted at the front of the hospital, it's

all close. What time do you need to have the girls back to Jake?'

'Around five. He's going to take them out once Letitia settles down for the night. Why?'

'I'd like to take you out to dinner before we head home.'

This wasn't likely to be a spur-of-the-moment invitation. She was sure he didn't do those. Which meant he'd thought this through and had still asked her out. On a date. Woo-hoo!

'Sounds great.' She fought to remain cool, calm and controlled. If he knew how excited she was, he'd probably run a mile.

Zac squeezed her hand, pulling her close and kissing her on the lips. 'See you soon.'

'Hello again.'

Evie had just paid for her nieces' ice creams and was putting her purse away when she heard Zac's voice. She looked up into his smiling face and greeted him with a smile in return.

'Hello yourself. How did the meeting go?'

'It's still going on.'

'Do you have to go back?'

'No. Greg Evans, the hospital CEO, is there. They don't need me.'

'It was a hospital meeting?'

'Plotting the future direction of the hospital. Very dull.' Zac squatted down to the level of Gracie and Mack and changed the topic. 'What have you seen?'

'The baby zebra,' said Mack.

'The ice creams,' said Gracie.

Zac laughed. 'You haven't seen the lions yet? They're my favourite.'

'We can go there now if you want,' Gracie said, holding out her little hand.

Mack checked the map. 'This way, past the flamingos.' Mack and Grace ran off, assuming the adults would follow.

Evie and Zac trailed behind, past the flamingos, the siamang monkeys and the sun bears, before finally reaching the lions' enclosure where the girls were delighting in the antics of the four cubs and their mother.

'Where are the daddy lions?' Gracie asked.

'I think they have to separate them from the cubs. I guess they'd be in another enclosure,' Evie replied. To Zac, she said, 'What is it you like about the daddy lions, to use Gracie's terminology?'

'What's not to like? What a great life, lazing about waiting to mate, lazing about some more while the lionesses make the kill. All without lifting a paw.'

Evie punched him lightly on the arm. 'I never pegged you for a chauvinist, Zac Carlisle!'

'That's quite a right hook,' he protested, rubbing his arm. 'If it's the politically correct answer you're after, then I grew up in a house just across the parklands and at night, lying in bed, I could hear the lions roar. I used to imagine I was on safari in Africa.' He stood for a moment, watching a cub who was stalking and pouncing on the twitching tail of one of the lionesses as she rested. 'One day,' he said, seemingly to himself, 'I'll get there.'

If he was going to divulge any more he was interrupted by the ringing of his mobile phone. 'Hello... Speaking... Where did you hear this information?'

He moved away but Evie wasn't out of earshot. She hadn't intended to eavesdrop but his tone suggested a problem and it didn't sound personal. Meaning she didn't try very hard not to listen.

'Yes, I was at the meeting... I can't confirm that. No decision has been made... I'm out of town at the moment. Can you hold the story until

I get back? I'd be happy to give you a statement when I'm back in Pelican Beach... Thank you.'

Zac came back to her and leant on the fencing around the big cat enclosure, drumming his fingers on the top rail. He didn't resume their conversation. The phone call had obviously unsettled him.

'What's going on?'

She half expected him to deflect her query but he answered her. 'It was one of the journos from the local paper, chasing a rumour that the nursing-home is being closed.'

'Our nursing-home?'

Zac nodded.

'Is it?'

'The government's cut our budget and we're having to look at options but no decision's been made.'

'You can't close it!'

'We might have to.'

'What about the residents?'

'Do you think we haven't thought of them? Nothing's final yet but what I didn't want was for people to go off half-cocked, which is exactly what will happen if this story gets out. I'll have to get back this afternoon to do some damage control.'

He was looking into the distance, his mind clearly already in Pelican Beach, ticking over, weighing up the situation.

'We'll drop the girls back with Jake and head off.'

He gave her a blank look, almost as if he'd forgotten she was there. 'You don't need to come. There's nothing you can do.'

'Except I need a lift home. I'm working tomorrow and Jake's not bringing the girls back until the evening. If you don't take me, I'm stuck.'

'OK, but we'll need to head off soon if I want a chance to set things straight. The paper comes out tomorrow.'

'Girls.' Evie called them over to her. 'It's time to head back to Dad. Race you to the meerkats on the way out?'

The girls led the way without argument and forty minutes later Evie and Zac were in the car, heading south. The radio was on and when one of her favourite songs was played Evie couldn't resist joining in.

'I love this song,' she said, singing along. Halfway through the first chorus she saw the look Zac gave her and he didn't seem captivated by her performance. 'Don't you like it?'

'I have no objection to the song…' Zac let his words trail off, implying his thoughts, too polite to voice his opinion.

Evie laughed. 'I know, I should only sing in the shower. But some songs just can't be ignored. How about I stop singing and you tell me about the meeting?'

It was clear Zac was battling with the options but, in the end, talking won over her vocals.

'What do you want to know?'

'You said you were plotting the future direction of the hospital. What does that mean?'

'We're trying to determine which services the hospital can and should offer. No final decision has been made. At least, it hadn't when I left the meeting today.'

'What were you discussing?'

Zac hesitated and Evie started humming softly, playing her trump card. When Zac smiled she said, 'You may as well tell me. Sounds like I'll be able to read about it in the paper tomorrow anyway.'

'But which version? That's what worries me.'

'What did the journo say?'

'He says his contact at Parliament House told him the nursing-home was being closed.'

'And is it?'

'I rang the CEO while you were dropping the girls back with Jake and the journo's source has got it wrong.'

'But you said yourself you were looking at options.'

'The government says they're cutting the health budget because they need the funds to meet their election promises for education. Today's meeting was about trying to convince the government not to reduce our budget.'

'Aren't governments always promising money for education *and* health?'

'Sure, but most of the people in our electorate vote for the opposition and the government isn't interested in catering for people who don't vote for them.'

'That's appalling.'

'It's a fact. Our bargaining power lies in organising unfavourable media coverage of their actions. That's why I need to put the lid on this story before it runs because although it could paint the government in an unfavourable light, it's just as likely the journo will put the negative spin on the hospital board. Whatever makes a story sensational.'

'Why were you at the meeting?'

'To give the medical view and to explain why we need those specific services and the funds to provide them.'

'What's going to happen?'

They were beyond the city limits now, driving past acres of vineyards as they wound their way through the start of the hills. Over Zac's shoulder, beyond the soft green of vineyards, Evie could see the sparkling waters of the Gulf of St Vincent, but the scenery went almost unnoticed as she concentrated on Zac's story.

'If our funding is reduced, we'll have to cut services. I was trying to show them that everything we currently provide is necessary. They wouldn't give us any straight answers and kept intimating we could do without the nursing-home. They can't actually make that decision but they must have voiced that thought if the journo heard about it. It's the only way I can see that this story has even got off the ground.'

'When do the proposed budget cuts come into effect?'

'In six weeks. And parliament doesn't resume until after that so it'll be difficult to get a result by then. We're hoping lobbying and media attention will work in our favour, but we haven't had time to put things into motion. We've been too busy sorting out staffing problems and looking at the finances.'

'What services are under threat?'

'The nursing-home, Day Surgery, Emergency or selling off the hospital housing.'

'Closing down the other departments?'

'Worst-case scenario.'

'You can't close Emergency!'

'We know. We could sell off the housing but that would only be a short-term solution to cash flow, and because the tenants do pay rent, it's a source of income for the hospital, albeit small.'

They'd reached the top of the hill and the road continued to wind down the other side, passing herds of dairy cows now rather than vineyards. Zac slowed down and steered his car towards the dirt verge as a teenage driver in a hotted-up utility, complete with spotlights and several radio antennae, overtook them, crossing a double white line in his attempt to get around them before the next corner. Evie watched him as he raced off down the hill, taking the corner far too wide and too fast.

'Bloody idiot,' Zac commented. 'That's why

we need an ED. Too many drivers doing stupid things on the road.'

Evie's mind was still on the crisis. 'What about Day Surgery?'

'That almost pays for itself so we wouldn't save much there. The nursing-home is heavily subsidised so it's an obvious one to privatize, but the board is reluctant.'

'You're not thinking of closing it?'

'No, but selling it off might happen.'

'Tough call.'

'Yeah, I know.'

As Zac negotiated the final bend in the road Evie noticed two black skid marks sliding off the road to their right. 'Someone didn't take the corner too well,' she said, as her eyes followed the line of the tyres. 'Oh, my God, Zac, pull over.'

Zac slammed on the brakes, pulling the car off the bitumen and onto the dirt verge. Checking for traffic, he swung the car in a U-turn before stopping beside a white roadside marker which had been snapped in two, presumably when it had been hit by the car, which was now resting, badly damaged, in a paddock beyond the road.

'Call triple-O, ask for the CFS, as well as the ambulance. Priority one. Tell them we're at the bottom of Willunga Hill, south side, where the road straightens out.'

She'd already reached for her phone and punched in the three zeros while Zac reached under his seat and pulled out a fire extinguisher. Climbing from the car, she checked the registration number for the operator so the emergency services could pinpoint their location. Zac had retrieved what Evie assumed to be a first-aid kit from the boot of his car and she quickly made her way to the wreck as soon as she had completed the call.

She looked at the vehicle's caved-in roof, its shattered windscreen, damaged when it must have rolled over, and the smashed spotlights. 'This looks like the car that passed us coming down the hill.'

Zac nodded. 'I reckon it is.' He'd walked around the ute and was still hanging onto the fire extinguisher and the first-aid kit. The paddock was quiet. The car's engine must have cut out in the accident, and there was no sound from within the utility's cab.

Zac wasn't trying to get to the driver. Why?

'Petrol tank doesn't seem to be leaking.' Zac put down the things he was holding and Evie realised he'd been checking for danger first. She knew the procedure—DR ABC. Danger, response, airway, breathing, circulation.

She didn't wait any longer. She was at the driver's door, banging on the window and calling out as she tried to open the door. Even as she pulled on the handle she knew she was wasting her energy—the roof was so badly dented there was no way the door would be able to open.

'We'll have to go through a window,' Zac said. The glass was crumpled, lines like a spider's web spreading across its entire surface, but it was still in place. Through it they could see the young driver, head slumped forward on his chest, unresponsive. 'I'll break the passenger window, but you'll have to slide in—I won't fit.' Zac didn't ask her if that was OK. They both knew she'd do it.

He handed her a pair of disposable gloves before picking up a rock and smashing the window, spraying the passenger seat with little squares of broken glass. Still not a flicker of movement from the driver. Evie tucked the gloves into her pocket and glanced at Zac. This didn't look good.

'Please, don't let him be dead,' Evie whispered.

Zac knocked out the last bits of glass clinging

to the window-frame and she scrambled inside, heedless of the glass strewn across the car.

'Check the steering-wheel, make sure there's no airbag.'

Evie hadn't given that a moment's thought but she'd heard stories of airbags going off after the event and the damage they could do. 'Doesn't seem to have one.'

She licked her fingers and stretched her hand out, holding her fingers under the boy's nose, waiting to feel him exhale. Was that a tiny puff of air? She couldn't see his chest rise and fall and she held her fingers under his nose for longer, wanting to make sure. Yes.

'He's still breathing.' So he still had a pulse, too. 'Hello. Can you hear me? You've been in an accident.'

Still nothing.

'We're not going to be able to get him out until the fire truck gets here. What injuries can you find?' Zac asked.

She pulled on the gloves and checked the boy out. 'He's got a swelling the size of a mango on his forehead. Broken wrist, right thigh is bleeding quite heavily. I think the door must have cut into him.'

'I'll pass you a torch. Check his pupils.'

Evie reached back to take the torch. She crouched in the seat, looking up at the boy, not wanting to move his head at all. She lifted one eyelid, shone the torch into his eye and watched the pupil constrict, then repeated the process on the other side. 'Right pupil is sluggish,' she reported. The possibility of a closed head injury didn't surprise either of them. The boy's loss of consciousness was showing no signs of lessening.

'Can you get a BP cuff on him?'

'Should be able to. His left arm seems OK.'

Zac dug out the blood-pressure cuff from his kit and passed it through the window. Evie wound it around the kid's arm, holding her breath as she waited for the reading.

'Eighty over fifty.'

'He needs to get to hospital. Where's the bloody CFS?'

They couldn't move him without the help of the Country Fire Service, but she could check if he was trapped anywhere else while they waited. She lay across the seats, running her hand down his legs. His feet were free and, apart from the wound on his right thigh, his legs seemed OK. But his stomach was quite distended—was abdominal bleeding the cause of his low blood pressure?

'His legs aren't trapped but he must have some internal bleeding. His stomach is tight.' He had to be bleeding from somewhere, she just couldn't find it.

'I can hear sirens,' Zac said.

'Did you hear?' she said to the boy. 'The ambulance is coming. We'll get you out and take you to hospital. You just have to hang in there.' Talking to him was all she could do for now. Maybe it wouldn't help but she had to try.

The ambulance and the fire truck arrived together and Zac pulled Evie out of the wreck once the officers made it to the car. The adrenaline that had flooded through her while she'd been in the car left her abruptly, leaving her legs like jelly. Unable to support her weight, she fell against Zac. He caught her and lowered her gently to the ground.

An ambulance officer wrapped a space blanket around her shoulders. 'Are you hurt?'

Evie shook her head, waving him away to help the boy while she sat, unneeded now, and watched the retrieval effort.

The CFS crew removed the smashed windscreen and peeled back the roof of the ute with the 'jaws of life,' leaving the car looking like a opened tin can. Evie could see Zac's lips moving but she couldn't hear anything over the noise of the rescue process. Someone was in the car where she had been, talking to the boy, wrapping a hard cervical collar around his neck. The boy was lifted out of the car on a Jordan frame, an oxygen mask over his face, and carried to the ambulance. He was still alive but didn't appear to have regained consciousness.

'I'm going in the ambulance—they need me.' Evie jumped at the sound of Zac's voice. She hadn't noticed him walk over. He squatted next to her. 'One of the CFS volunteers will drive you home in my car. Will you be OK?'

She nodded silently. Of course he'd go in the ambulance. He was a doctor after all, more qualified than anyone else there. Which left her with nothing to do. She wasn't needed any more. She struggled to her feet before Zac could help her. She was OK. She was fine.

A few minutes later, Evie was sitting in Zac's car, a stranger next to her in the driver's seat, watching the ambulance speed away, lights flashing, siren screaming, as she thought about the boy in the back. The boy who was so close to death. So young and his life in the balance.

Would he make it?

Evie couldn't settle. She lay on the couch and tried to read but her mind kept wandering. The house was too quiet, with Jake and the girls away in Adelaide, too empty. She'd spoken to Letitia on the phone and everything was well with her but Evie felt restless, frustrated.

She'd felt like that since the ambulance had driven away, taking Zac and the injured boy.

She'd wanted to be the one in the ambulance, to be useful, and the fact she hadn't been grated on her nerves. How was the boy going? No one would tell her anything over the phone but all she had to do was walk over to the hospital and she'd know. Instead, she was wandering around the house, feeling irritated.

She'd persuaded herself she should stay home as she'd showered and was in her pyjamas but it didn't take much effort to throw a pair of trousers on over a singlet top and boxer shorts. Finally deciding that being at home on her own wasn't the answer, she went to grab some other clothes. She had one leg in her cargo pants when there was a knock on the door. She pulled them on then went to answer the door.

'Zac.' He was on her doorstep. He looked exhausted, his face was pale, the shadow of his stubble a contrast to the pallor of his skin, his thick hair more dishevelled than usual, and he wasn't smiling.

'He didn't make it.'

The boy in the ute. Gone. No more dreams. No more plans. Dead. Just like that.

She tugged at Zac's hand, pulling him inside and into her arms. He accepted her embrace and enveloped her in his arms in return. They stood, joined together, silent, comforting each other.

'Sometimes I hate my job.' Zac spoke first, breaking the moment, breaking the embrace.

'Come with me.' Evie led him through the house to the lounge. For the first time that night she was grateful she had the house to herself. She led him to the couch, making him sit, her earlier unsettled wanderings forgotten now she had a purpose.

She went to the kitchen and searched Jake's pantry until she found a bottle of brandy. She had no idea what it was like, Jake probably only used it for cooking but it didn't matter. Zac needed a drink of something. She screwed up her nose at the smell as the golden liquid splashed into the tumbler.

She carried it to Zac, who glanced at it briefly before swallowing it in one gulp.

'What happened?'

Zac put his glass on the coffee-table and rubbed his hands over his face. Hard.

'Mark had a collapsed lung. We got to that, but he had massive internal injuries, haemorrhaging everywhere. It was too much. His heart gave out. We just watched him die.'

Evie held one of his hands in hers. 'I'm sure you did everything you could. It's not your fault.'

'Just because it wasn't my fault doesn't make it easier to deal with.'

'You weren't making him drive so recklessly and you certainly didn't make him roll his car. You did everything you could to help.'

'But it wasn't enough.'

'From the sound of it, no one would have been able to do any more. At least he didn't die alone in his car in some paddock.'

'I wish he hadn't died at all.'

'Death is part of life, Zac, and part of medicine. What's bothering you? Is there something different about Mark's death?'

Zac was leaning forward, shoulders slumped, his hands buried in his thick hair. 'He was the same age as Clare was when she died. Almost exactly the same age.'

His words were muffled by his posture and Evie wasn't sure if she'd heard correctly. 'Clare?'

'My sister.'

Evie hesitated and then asked her question, tentatively, in case her concern wasn't welcome. 'What happened?'

'She had cystic fibrosis and she died when I was sixteen. She missed her eighteenth birthday by ten days. Mark would have turned eighteen in a week's time.'

The pain in Zac's voice was raw. She squeezed his hand but said nothing. Saying she was sorry, the only words she had, would be useless to him.

'I miss her. She fought as hard as she could, she was unfailingly brave, but there was nothing we could do.' Zac took a deep breath before clenching his jaw. Evie took him into her arms. 'She was too young to die.'

Evie kissed his forehead gently, pressing her lips to his skin, using her touch to soothe him, offering comfort. What other way was there when words were useless?

CHAPTER SEVEN

EVIE was skittish the following morning, her emotions in turmoil. The happiness she'd experienced when she'd been in Zac's arms had been dampened by the overwhelming sadness she'd felt as she'd listened to him talk about his sister. She was walking through the hospital in a world of her own and only looked into the staffroom by chance, her attention drawn by virtue of the extraordinary amount of noise emanating from the room. Judging by the throng around the coffee-machine, something was afoot.

'What's up?' Evie joined the group.

'You haven't seen the local rag?' Evie shook her head in response to the question from Claudia, another RN. 'The rumours were spreading like wildfire yesterday that the nursing-home was being closed. Tom did his best to stamp them out but it's all here in black and white.' She waved the paper she was holding before passing it to Evie, who stepped away to read the article.

It wasn't hard to find—it was the feature headline on page one. *Nursing-Home Shock.* Followed in slightly smaller print with *City doctor leaves own aunt homeless.*

What she read confused and infuriated her.

Zac Carlisle, GP and board member of Pelican Beach Hospital, yesterday offered 'No comment' in response to news of the imminent closure of the nursing-home where his frail and elderly aunt has been a resident for a number of years.

Our sources confirmed the home will be closed, leaving dozens of elderly residents stranded. With no other facility in the local area, residents will be forced to relocate long distances away, putting them out of contact with friends and family—and with their friends within the home. Our investigation yesterday confirmed long waiting lists at all of the State's nursing-homes contacted, with some even refusing to take any more applications.

The paper dropped out of her hand onto the coffee-table, landing with a flutter that echoed her unsteady heartbeat.

What was she meant to make of that?

She tuned back into a conversation on the other side of the room. There seemed to be a split, with two of the staff arguing that the report was definitely true and fitted stories they'd heard of the extra time Zac had been seen in the nursing-home admin area—what had he been doing there if the paper wasn't right? A third person argued they couldn't know one way or another until the board had made a formal announcement.

Evie slipped away. It was nearly time for her shift to start. It might be hours until she had a break so she'd have to wait to find answers to her questions. She needed Zac—or did she? She'd asked him for answers yesterday and he'd told her there had been no decision. Had he lied? Or had the journalist got the facts wrong? And how did she work out whom to believe?

The emergency department was busy, as it often was at seven in the morning, before the medical clinics opened their doors and took some of the pressure off the hospital. But the emergencies hardly qualified as such—a greenstick fracture of an arm that needed a cast, a baby with a very high temperature and vomiting who needed fluids and intravenous anti-nausea medication and an elderly gentleman with chest pains who responded to GTN spray.

Unfortunately the straightforward nursing care allowed Evie plenty of time to run though all the different scenarios for the story in the paper. The moment her morning teabreak started she headed for the nursing-home, determined to see for herself just what the situation was.

The first person she bumped into outside the nursing-home was Lexi.

'Evie! I'm glad I ran into you. Are we still on tonight?'

'Tonight?' Evie paused, her mind was so completely occupied with the rumours she couldn't even think what day of the week it was. Friday, their TV show. 'I'll have to let you know, but do you have a minute now?'

'About the nursing-home?'

'How did you guess?'

'It's all anyone's talking about, and as Tom is my husband, and he's on the board, people think I'm in the loop.'

'Are you?'

'I think it's best I stay out of it, actually, but I'll tell you this. As far as I'm aware, no decision has been made about the nursing-home.'

'Then the article?'

Lexi shrugged. 'Who knows where that came from. But it's caused a lot of anxiety. I'm here now because I had to give Mrs Kale a sedative to calm her down.'

'Why isn't the board saying anything?'

'Zac and Tom have both been here, trying to allay the residents' fears, and I know they're both pretty stressed. Their priority is speaking to the residents, not to the public. The CEO is in Adelaide and not due back until tomorrow. I think the paper contacted him but his reaction isn't as newsworthy as Zac's, because of Fel's involvement. I'm afraid the focus has fallen on Zac and he's doing his best, Evie. That's all I know. I have to run. Call me later, OK?'

'Sure.' Evie headed in the opposite direction, walking quickly. She knew where she was going, she just didn't know what she was going to find.

The last thing she expected to see was a small brawl between the residents over who would be interviewed by the journalists who were apparently due to descend at any moment. Despite the arguing, the mood was one of excitement.

Zac was nowhere to be seen. Pam, the diversional therapist, was attempting to restore order amidst the rising pitch of the discussions, and in the midst of the chaos, Fel and Nancy sat calmly, looking like they knew a great big secret.

She knew who to speak to. 'What are you up to?'

They chuckled. 'I know I'm "frail and elderly",' Fel quoted the article, 'but I have a few tricks up my sleeve yet.'

'Did one of you speak to that journalist yesterday?'

'Absolutely not,' said Nancy.

'Then how did he know about the connection between Fel and Zac?'

The glint in Fel's eye caught Evie's attention and she fixed the elderly woman with a look. 'I might have had a few words when he came calling,' Fel admitted.

'You never!' Nancy was horrified.

'It's for the best, you old worry wart. How are we going to get what we want if we don't give them a whiff of scandal? The papers won't be interested unless they have a hook, and without coverage we're not going to get the publicity we need to turn this nursing-home fiasco around.'

'But he's your nephew!' Nancy said, clearly scandalised but, Evie suspected, enjoying herself immensely.

'Great-nephew,' corrected Fel, 'and what he doesn't know won't hurt him.'

'But, but...' Evie was lost for words. She stopped and took stock of the situation. 'Is this nursing-home closing or not?'

'Zac assures us nothing's definite but we also hadn't been told anything for sure until yesterday when the journalist started fishing around. So I took a punt that where there's smoke there's fire and did some damage control.'

'More like fanning the flames, Fel,' said Evie, her voice dry.

At least she knew where the link to Zac had come from. But where had the story started in the first place? And was it true? She still didn't know.

'What are they all arguing about TV crews for?' Evie indicated the other residents nearby.

'You're tenacious, young lady,' said Fel with approval. 'You'll be a good match for Zac.'

Evie sniffed. 'I don't want someone who throws people out of their homes.'

'Ha! So you want him if this story isn't true! Excellent,' said Nancy, rubbing her hands.

She felt a blush creep across her throat but she wasn't admitting to anything. Besides, if Zac had lied to her, that would be it. It would be over before it had started. She forced her attention back to the nursing-home drama. 'Can we focus on the issue?' She wasn't sure which of them she was admonishing. 'TV crews?'

'The reporter from the weeknight current affairs programme in Adelaide is coming down in a few hours to get some interviews. Everyone wants to be on the telly.'

'And? Why aren't you over there, staking your claim?'

'We've already got it stitched up.'

'How?' Should she be disapproving of this? All she felt was amusement, which was increasing by the second.

'The reporter phoned me direct as I was named in the paper this morning. He's interviewing Zac first, then me. Zac doesn't know about my part yet. I've promised Nancy I'll share my screen time with her.'

Nancy patted her short curls into place. 'It's our fifteen minutes, we're going to make the most of it.'

'Come and watch—we'll page you,' Fel invited.

'I finish at three. I'll come by then and see what you're up to. Jake is bringing the girls back today and staying overnight so I'll have a bit of time straight after work.'

'You should be using you free time to enslave Zac.'

'I'm officially ignoring you. Is there any point in telling you two to stay out of trouble?'

'None at all,' said Fel, her face wreathed in smiles.

'Only if it makes you feel better,' added Nancy. 'But it won't do much else.'

Would it make her feel better? she wondered as she left the two women to go back to work.

She doubted it, but not because of any sense of disapproval over their antics.

From the little curl of excitement in the pit of her belly, she had a sneaking suspicion that if only she found out Zac hadn't lied, she was actually enjoying the drama as much Fel and Nancy.

At three-thirty Evie was back at the nursing-home. The common room looked like a movie set. Silver reflective light shades were angled down at two couches which had been repositioned, Evie assumed, to suit the programme's director. Zac was seated at one end of a couch, immaculate in a grey pinstriped suit, white shirt and a blue-grey tie knotted perfectly at his throat. Even the yellowing bruise around his eye had been disguised with make-up and the contrast to his normal rumpled appearance was astonishing. At the other end of the couch sat a woman who was dressed in a black suit, her hair coiffed and perfect, her mouth a slash of red lipstick. The sound equipment was being held aloft over her head, the camera was rolling and the woman was chattering away nineteen to the dozen while a man Evie took to be the interviewer was seated off camera, apparently waiting to speak. Evie watched for a minute, waiting to hear Zac's comments before realising he'd be lucky to get a word in. The woman clearly loved the limelight.

'We are appalled at the government's plans to radically slash funding to our rural areas, forcing hospitals to close, turning out elderly residents from nursing-homes,' the woman was saying. Evie tuned out, her attention focussed on Zac,

who didn't appear to have seen her yet. That was
not the face of a man who did unkind things was
all she could think. 'This flies in the face of their
election promises and shows once again why this
government is not to be trusted.'

Evie noticed Nancy and Fel sitting in one corner
of the common room, also watching proceedings.
They were being so uncharacteristically quiet she
hadn't spotted them immediately. They motioned
her over, both of them beaming with pleasure.
'It's a political bun fight we've landed in—isn't
it wonderful!' Fel whispered, drawing a glare and
a shake of the head from the sound technician.

They fell silent, listening to the interview,
although Evie was sure they were stifling giggles
at having been told off like schoolgirls.

'Thank you for being with us today, Ms
Knapman.' The woman added her thanks and the
focus swung to the reporter. 'Shadow Minister
for Health, Ms Victoria Knapman, at the Pelican
Beach Nursing-Home.'

Ah, so that's why Fel had mentioned politics.

'And also with us is Dr Carlisle.' He went on
to describe Zac's position at the hospital. 'Dr
Carlisle, with the board of the hospital, has been
blamed by the local residents for closing the

nursing-home without community consultation. Your response, Doctor?'

'The government has hit the hospital with a raft of unpalatable funding cuts and is still undertaking a lengthy inspection process aimed at enforcing even more cuts.' His voice was calm and deep and thrilled Evie with its quiet assurance. Zac was commanding. 'I will reiterate that the board has not made a final decision on what steps will be taken to accommodate those shortfalls in funding. Closure of the nursing-home is an option but one that will be taken only as a last resort.'

'Do you have any response to claims you issued a statement of "No comment" yesterday to the *Pelican Beach Weekly*?'

'I was phoned when I was out of town, which I explained, and said I would contact the reporter later that day when I returned. Unfortunately I was waylaid by a medical emergency and by the time I was free, the story had already been filed.'

'And what of the reports claiming your aunt is in the home?'

'She is indeed. Another reason why, contrary to rumour, I will do everything in my power to ensure the home remains in operation, for her sake and for the sake of all the residents.'

Filming stopped. Zac's interview was finished and attention turned to Fel and Nancy who, within minutes, were being seated on the couch, obviously trying to decide whether to ham up the frail and elderly angle or put their best camera faces on. The shadow minister hovered, looking for more minutes of camera time, but Zac seemed eager to get out of there.

He was crossing the room at a rapid pace and Evie thought for a moment he wasn't going to stop to talk to her—hadn't he seen her?

'Zac,' she called out to him, and he looked startled, almost guilty. Had he been intending to walk straight past her?

'Evie.' His voice alone was enough to send shivers of excitement through her. Deep and rich, it was the perfect voice for a big man.

'So the paper did get it wrong?'

'The background was right but their conclusions weren't accurate, which was what I was worried about. With the accident, I didn't get to the journalist, if he deserves the title, until too late.' He paused, checking his watch. 'I have to get over to the surgery, I've got a clinic starting in a few minutes, but could you come over tonight, about eight? I need to see you.'

'Eight it is.' She watched Fel and Nancy's interview but wouldn't have been able to tell anyone what they said, she was too caught up in making plans for the evening. Everything was okay. Last night she'd been afraid he'd use Clare's death to pull away again. And today, she'd been confronted with the fact that he might have lied to her about the nursing-home. Her fears had been put to rest on both points. There was every reason for tonight to be perfect.

Zac stripped his shirt off as he walked through his front door. Five past eight already. Did he have time for a quick shower? He threw his shirt into the laundry and was bending down to untie his shoelaces when he heard a knock at the door. Evie.

'It's open,' he called, slipping his shoes off, throwing his socks into the laundry basket and padding in bare feet out to the kitchen. He froze in the doorway. Evie was standing in the kitchen, her back to him, obviously wondering where he was.

She wore a skirt that sat low on her hips and swirled about her legs in a riot of bright colours and her feet were clad in soft red shoes that wrapped about her ankles. A large expanse of smooth creamy skin was on display beneath a tiny top. Shiny bangles adorned her arms and glittered in the light as she flicked her dark hair over her shoulders, sending it tumbling down her slender back. She turned slightly and he caught a glimpse of her face in profile. Her cheeks were flushed, her eyes huge and dark. She was gorgeous and he felt his body's unbidden response to her presence. He fought his desire to gather her into his arms.

For a man who'd sworn off relationships he'd spent an awful lot of time thinking about this woman. This woman standing before him, an arm's length away, half-dressed while he was half-naked. It took all his self-control to remain in the doorway.

'Evie.' His voice was hoarse, choked with raw emotion.

She turned to face him and he saw her register his bare chest, watched her gaze travel down over his hips and back to his face. Saw her swallow and blush. Again he fought the desire to close the distance between them and take her in his arms. But Evie didn't hesitate. She took that step, stopping an inch from him, raising one hand and placing it over his heart. He closed his eyes, focussing on the pressure of her fingers on his skin, lost in the shivers he felt coursing through his body.

He couldn't afford to lose control, but this was too much. He couldn't resist her, couldn't fight it.

The world didn't exist except for Evie.

Nothing else mattered.

There was nothing else. Nothing except wanting her.

He gave in to his desire, pulling her close, and together they dived into a world where nothing else existed except their mutual need.

'That was amazing.' And it had been. Deliciously, mind-blowingly, incredibly amazing.

Zac looked dazed. She knew the feeling but— was it more than that? He seemed disorientated.

She sat up and grabbed for the sheet that was tangled at the foot of the bed, suddenly feeling vulnerable. Zac raised himself up, too, on one arm, his biceps straining under the weight of his upper body. The distance between them widened.

'What's wrong?' Did she want to know? But she had to ask, she couldn't bear the strained silence that had sprung up between them.

'That shouldn't have happened, Evie. I knew it but I wanted you so badly I let myself forget.'

'Then you can keep forgetting.'

Zac shook his head. 'This can't happen.'

'It just did.' Evie scrunched the corner of the sheet up in her hand. Her heart was pounding, nervousness taking over.

'But it can't happen again. I'm not looking for a relationship, commitment.'

'Who said anything about commitment?' Evie wasn't certain she was following this. How could he share that experience with her and then say it wouldn't happen again? 'We have unbelievable chemistry, we can explore that without having to make a major commitment.'

Zac shook his head. 'I can't do that.'

Evie reached out to him but he shied away from her touch. 'Let go a bit, Zac, live in the moment. You miss so much if you don't.'

'It's not about the moment. It's about the future.'

'The future will take care of itself. Don't miss out on what you've got right now by worrying about the future.'

'You don't understand, Evie. If we go down that path, if we explore this chemistry, then before you know it we'll be in a relationship and you'll want commitment.'

'Even if you're right, what's so wrong with

that?' The sheet, pulled up to her shoulders, was down low on Zac's side, leaving too much of his tempting abdomen on display.

'Commitment means marriage and babies—I'm not doing that again.'

'What do you mean, "again"?'

'I've been married before. We didn't have the happy ever after I was hoping for.'

'And babies?'

Zac's voice faltered. 'A daughter.'

'You have a daughter?'

Zac shook his head.

'I'm not following you.' She waited for Zac to explain.

Would he? She doubted it, but she needed to know. And after last night she was entitled to an explanation, she was entitled to know why he was pulling away.

He hesitated, then started to talk, the words rushing out as though a dam had burst. 'We started out so sure of ourselves, convinced our love would get us through anything, but when everything was thrown at us, it was more than our marriage could handle.'

'I think you'd better start at the beginning.'

'The beginning is Clare.'

'Your sister?'

Zac nodded. 'Clare had cystic fibrosis but I'm a carrier.'

'One CF gene and one normal?'

Zac nodded. 'When Gabby and I got married, we knew we wanted a family. We talked about all the possibilities we faced, given I was a carrier of CF. I wanted Gabby to be tested as well, but she refused. Our families had known each other all our lives. Gabby knew as much about CF as I did and she said it wouldn't matter—no parents would be better able to cope than us. I went along with her, against my better instincts, because I loved her.'

'Gabby fell pregnant and then she started to panic. I tried to calm her, reminded her of our promises to each other, but she couldn't cope with the thought of a child with special needs. She had chorionic villus sampling and the baby, a girl, tested positive for CF.'

'Gabby wanted an abortion. To me, that wasn't an option. She was beside herself but agreed to see a genetic counsellor with me. In the end, she didn't wait. She went ahead with the termination. I only knew about it afterwards.'

He was hunched over now, his arms wrapped

around his knees, closed to her and, oh, so changed from just a few hours ago. 'In different ways I lost my sister, my daughter and my wife to cystic fibrosis. Our marriage disintegrated, we couldn't hold it together after that.' He exhaled a harsh breath, closing his eyes for a moment and rubbing at them vigorously with the back of his hand, blinking hard when he opened them again. 'I don't blame Gabby. I should have insisted she get tested before we tried for a baby. One in twenty-two people carry the gene for CF and it wasn't unreasonable to think she might. I didn't insist on testing but now I know better.'

'You were both carriers so you each have one faulty, or CF, gene and one normal, right?' Evie asked. Zac nodded. 'So even if you knew you were both carriers, then that wouldn't automatically mean a baby, any baby, you had would have the disease, would it? They might just be a carrier or not even a carrier.'

'But if we were both carriers, there would have been a one in four chance a child would inherit a faulty gene from both of us and have CF. Bad odds. I know you're trying to understand, but what you really need to understand is why I can't commit again. People make all sorts of promises in good faith. Gabby and I both did. We promised to love each other through good and bad, in sickness and in health but when reality hit, we couldn't do it.'

She put a tentative hand on his arm and he didn't shrug it off. Which was better than nothing but not as good as what she really wanted—a repeat of last night and not to be having this conversation into which he was putting all his effort to convince her they couldn't be together. 'I'm really sorry, Zac, for your losses.' She hesitated—was she pushing too far? Probably, but she didn't want to accept he was ending this. It was still too much to believe he could consider it, after last night. 'But you and Gabby are only two people—that doesn't make it true for everyone. Some people make it through the tough times.'

If he'd heard her, he didn't let on, hell-bent on drumming his reality into her head. 'We weren't able to keep those promises under pressure and it's unrealistic to think anyone does. So now I don't ask people to make promises to me and I don't make promises. We don't know how strong we are until we're put under pressure. The one thing I do know is I'm not strong enough to cope with any more loss.

'My daughter would have been almost three now, running around, talking, throwing her arms about me, driving me crazy with her mess. I can't go there again. So the best solution for me, the only solution, is not to get involved in the first place.'

Evie started to speak but Zac placed a finger across her lips. 'I know what you're going to say but, please, understand, I've been through every scenario myself, many times. I've made a decision. I'm sticking by it.'

He climbed from the bed and crossed the room, stark naked. Evie heard the shower and briefly entertained the idea of joining him, but she knew any attempt to dissuade him at this point would be futile. She waited. And waited. The water kept running. He was staying in there until he was sure she'd gone. There was only one thing to do. Take the hint and leave before he came out of the bathroom.

CHAPTER EIGHT

HE DIDN'T do commitment.

He didn't want it and even if he did, it wasn't a possibility, not with his background.

He'd made that decision three years ago and hadn't had any trouble sticking with it. Until he'd met Evie. Now he was having trouble thinking about anything else.

He hadn't told anyone, other than his family, about what had happened to his marriage. He'd needed to tell Evie. Had to make sure she understood, that she'd respect his need to keep his distance.

But, try as he may he was having trouble blocking Evie out of his mind and his mother, who was spending the weekend at her holiday house, wasn't helping.

'So, who is this Evie I keep hearing about from Fel?'

'She's a nurse at the hospital, she lives next

door.' If he kept her neatly compartmentalised—colleague, neighbour—maybe he'd manage. If he could keep the lid on the compartment labelled 'intoxicating, belly-dancing gypsy,' maybe he'd survive.

'Fel seems to have taken quite a shine to her.'

His mother had a gift for making her questions sound like statements. He thought about ignoring her but knew he wouldn't get away with it.

'Evie and Fel are like peas in a pod, outspoken and impetuous.'

'Not your type, then?' His mother was watching him carefully and he wondered just what Fel had said. 'When do I get to meet her?'

'You don't.' Any further comments he felt like making about his mother's insatiable curiosity were put on hold by the appearance of a pair of smiling little girls at his back door.

As he stood up to open the door he said, 'But you can meet the next best things.' Gracie and Mack scampered in, pulling up short when they saw his mother. 'Gracie, Mack, this is my mum, Mrs Carlisle. Mum, these two young ladies are my next-door neighbours.' He paused for effect. 'Evie is their aunt.'

His mum was all smiles, standing up to shake their hands as she greeted them, which apparently earned her immediate approval from the girls. 'And what brings you here today?'

'It was a 'mergency,' said Gracie.

'An emergency,' clarified Mack.

Gracie nodded, her little face, so like her aunt's, set earnestly.

'Evie is going to cook,' added Mack.

'Ah,' said Zac. 'Say no more.'

'And that means she's about to start singing, too.'

'You're right, there was nothing for it but to escape.'

A knock at the front door had Gracie and Mack in a panic. 'She's found us!' squealed Gracie, as she ducked under the kitchen table, dragging Mack with her. Both were giggling furiously, finding it all a huge joke.

'Seems like I came by at an opportune moment,' said his mum. 'Are you going to invite them to join us for lunch?'

Squeals of 'Yay!' from the girls followed him up the hallway. Lunch was a popular idea.

Evie stood on the doorstep, fidgeting with the hem of her T-shirt, and he was sure she was avoiding his gaze just as he was trying to do the same. 'Did the girls come?' She broke off, raising her eyes heavenwards as she heard the giggling.

'Come in. They're in the kitchen.'

Evie followed him down the passageway, coming to an abrupt halt when she saw his mother.

'Sorry, I didn't realise you had company.'

His mother laughed and stood up to introduce herself. 'I'm hardly company, I'm Zac's mum, Lydia. You must be Evie. I'm very pleased to meet you.'

Evie shook Lydia's hand, looking a little puzzled.

'She's just met the girls,' Zac said, trying to explain how his mother knew of her.

'Are you going to join us for lunch?' Zac could have throttled his mother. After the past thirty-six hours he and Evie had had, he didn't need the added complication of the two of them getting chummy. Having Fel in Evie's corner was bad enough; he knew his mother would like her, too. Everybody did.

'I can't do that.' Good. Evie didn't want the complication either.

'Yes, you can. I insist.' Evie didn't look too thrilled about the idea, but as the girls weren't coming out from underneath the table and it was obvious his mother wasn't going to take no for an answer, she didn't have much choice.

Within five minutes Evie clearly had his mother's approval and after half an hour Zac was wondering if they'd even notice if he left the table so engrossed were they in their conversation. They'd scarcely looked at their lunch as they'd eaten and Evie hadn't given any clue that she was even aware of Zac, much less upset or angry with him. Good at pretending? Or was this what she'd meant by living in the moment—and at this moment she was talking with his mum?

Gracie and Mack had run off to play with the world globe, leaving him to sit and listen as the two women held an intense discussion on various aspects of fundraising. His mum was passionate about the topic and had been heavily involved in fundraising for the Cystic Fibrosis Council for years—but Evie?

It didn't take long for him to find the connection.

'Lydia, what do you think about the prospects of pulling together a fundraising event for the nursing-home? Not a black-tie sort of affair like you hold, more like a community fête on as large a scale as possible.' Her eyes were alight with

interest, she was leaning in towards Lydia, engrossed in their conversation, alive and sparkling. In a nutshell, captivating.

'Anything is possible if you want it enough,'
Lydia said with a glance in Zac's direction. What
was that about? 'When are you thinking?'

'A week? Two?'

His mum had to be baulking at the idea of such
a short time-frame but she didn't miss a beat,
just nodded and continued talking. He knew Evie
was spontaneous but there was no way she could
pull off an event like that in that time. She wasn't
even from here, she had no contacts.

'I don't think my son agrees with me, though,
judging from the frown on his face.'

He'd been sprung. 'I don't want to rain on your
parade, but what's your aim?' Coming up with
objections wasn't a smart move after everything
that had happened, but he had to be honest. 'If the
home is privatised, this is all academic, and you
can't raise enough to cover the ongoing costs and
enable us to keep it as part of the hospital.'

'There's no point waiting to see how it all pans
out, it's too late by then,' Evie countered, speaking
directly to him for the first time since she'd sat
down. 'Why not show the community is behind

the home and we're all willing to make sure it stays? Won't that give you more ammunition to go to the media with, to embarrass the government into doing the right thing?'

His mother was on Evie's side. 'You were right, Zac. Evie is a lot like Fel, brimful of ideas and not afraid to make them happen.'

'You said that about me?' He nodded as she looked at him consideringly, but she said nothing further.

'Shall we go next door and make some plans?' Lydia suggested to Evie, and without waiting for Zac's reaction they rose from the table. 'Zac, you'll look after the girls while Evie and I get the ball rolling?'

He wasn't going to be left at the table by himself without putting his two cents in. 'Evie, are you seriously telling me that in the last hour you've committed to the idea of a fundraiser, just like that? And, Mum, you see no problems with it?'

'Nothing that can't be surmounted.'

Evie responded at the same time. 'Not just like that. I've been mulling over solutions to the hospital's financial problems and then I meet your mum and it turns out she's an expert in the art of fundraising. Besides, I don't want to be accused of being too spontaneous.' She tossed her dark waves of hair back from her shoulders, the gesture almost inviting him to challenge her. 'So I'm thinking it'll be today fortnight, rather than in a week.'

'A huge concession,' he said, smiling at last. This was exactly like Evie after all, and it was what he liked about her. And, as unbelievable as it all sounded, he'd wager she'd pull the whole thing off.

She was an incredible woman.

Just not for him.

Evie glanced around at the crowd in the nursing-home common room. It had been a crazy evening. The babysitter had been running late, Gracie had had a stomachache and hadn't wanted Evie to leave, she'd heard Zac in his garden, talking on the phone, and had delayed leaving until he'd gone inside. All in all, it had been an effort to arrive on time for the meeting and to arrive calm and unflustered.

She'd liaised with the television crew, who'd returned for more footage, keen on the 'community' aspect to the story, and was now waiting for the final few people to find their seats. The general

turnout looked promising and the mood was ener-
gised.

The extra commitment of spearheading the
fundraising project had turned out to be a blessing,
filling in the last spare moments of time she had
in her busy schedule and stopping her from
dwelling on Zac. The initial success made her feel
a little less of a failure for messing up so badly.

Young and old had turned out to help and there
was enough enthusiasm in the room to make her
believe anything was possible. Even the mayor
had promised to arrange the relevant council
permits to enable the fair to take place on the
town's foreshore. Amazing what the presence of
a camera could do.

After welcoming everybody, Evie divided
people into what she hoped were workable com-
mittees, groups of people who'd get along and get
on with the job, then she gave a short interview
to the television crew, doing her best to deliver
sound bites that would encapsulate their cause in
short, snappy statements.

Two hours later all the groups seemed well on
the way to having firm plans for the event and
Evie had a main committee organised to oversee
the general set-up.

'I think I've delegated all my responsibilities,' she said to Fel as the last few people left the room.

'Then you're a natural leader.'

'Let's wait and see how it all turns out. I should get to work and you must be exhausted.'

'I slept all afternoon in preparation. We haven't had so much fun here in ages and if they're going to close us down, we're going out with a bang.'

'It's not going to happen,' Evie said, trying to sound upbeat and positive. 'I've even got the shadow minister's secretary saying she'll be here for the fête. I know she doesn't give a damn about this—she's after the publicity and she'd attend the opening of an envelope—but it's a good issue for the opposition and guarantees us more coverage.'

'And more coverage is more leverage. You keep working that charm and you'll have us all safe in our beds yet.'

Safe in her bed wasn't what she wanted. It was Zac in her bed that would make her happy. But according to him, it wasn't going to happen again. Ever.

Ever was a long time to wait for the best sex she'd ever had to be repeated.

Ever wasn't going to cut it.

* * *

Night shift at Pelican Beach Hospital was often busy during summer, Evie had been told, as it was peak tourist season. Two hours into her stint, when she'd only seen one patient, she feared it wasn't going to be one of those nights. And she needed to keep busy. She couldn't make miracles happen at work, and it was a miracle she needed to put things right between her and Zac. So she needed to keep her mind off Zac—or his bed to be precise.

She checked the doctor's roster, just in case she needed to call for assistance. She should have expected as much—Zac was on call. She should be grateful it was so quiet she didn't need to work with him tonight. But the empty department left her with too much time to think. Which meant, of course, she thought about Zac.

At one-thirty in the morning Evie saw her second patient for the shift, a twenty-four-year-old woman who was convinced she had appendicitis. Fortunately, on examination, the woman's stomach pain turned out to be nothing more than abdominal cramps that eased with muscle relaxants. Evie breathed a sigh of relief. She'd handled it on her own and there'd been no need to call Zac.

Her relief was short-lived. An hour later she took a panicked phone call.

'My wife's in labour. What do I do?'

'How many weeks is she?'

'Thirty-six.'

'Is it her first baby?'

'Yes.' Evie relaxed. The pains could very well turn out to be Braxton-Hicks' contractions and, if not, she should have time to call Zac and direct the couple to the birthing suite in the hospital.

'How far apart are her contractions?'

'Not very.' Not the most helpful of answers. 'My wife says she wants to push!'

Damn. It sounded like the real thing, she wasn't going to be able to divert them. 'How far away are you?'

'Five minutes.'

'Tell your wife to pant, little breaths. Get here as quickly as you can. I'll meet you in front of Emergency.'

Evie hung up the phone and concentrated on what she needed to organise, all the issues with Zac pushed to one side. She called the medical wards and confirmed they had extra staff on night shift and could bring her a humidicrib. They would also alert the helicopter retrieval team in Adelaide to be on standby and call Zac, leaving her free to check the size of the suction tubing on hand, connecting the smallest diameter one she had available, sized for a neonate. Oxygen was no problem. She just hoped she'd be able to get the expectant mother into the emergency department. She didn't fancy delivering a baby in a car.

Slipping on a fresh gown, she grabbed two pairs of surgical gloves and pushed a barouche out to the ambulance bay, scanning the street for the headlights of the car. She was ready.

A figure emerged from the darkness, jogging towards her. Zac. Even in the darkness she recognised him, and her body recognised him, too. Her heart rate escalated, her breaths came more rapidly and she felt the familiar tingle run through her. He was in casual clothes, a cobalt-blue polo shirt and cotton trousers, his hair tousled from sleep. The tingle intensified. She stamped on it, firmly, and got in touch with her wounded pride. It wasn't hard.

'Evie!' He sounded surprised to see her. She'd forgotten it hadn't been her who'd paged him. He stopped beside her and she breathed in his scent of warm bed, fresh sheets and mint. She didn't want to think of warm beds!

'What have we got?'

He was all business. She could be, too. 'Primigravida at thirty-six weeks. She's ready to push. No other information. They should be here any minute.' She pulled on her gloves, handing him the second pair. He pulled them on, covering his long fingers, evoking sensations she didn't want to remember. She turned away, pretending to be absorbed in watching the driveway.

Headlights. Excellent. She could get her mind back on the job.

A car screeched to a halt in front of the emergency entrance. A distressed young man almost fell out of the driver's seat in his haste to get out of the car. Lying on the back seat, knees flexed, her hair soaked in sweat, was his pregnant wife. Evie quickly introduced herself and Zac to the couple, Steve and Caroline, before Zac started his examination. The external lights of the hospital gave out enough power to light the back seat.

'I can see the baby's head.'

Thank God it wasn't breech.

Zac gave her a thumbs-up. 'The cord's clear.'

'You're doing really well, Caroline. We're going to transfer you to a bed and get you inside, then you can push,' Evie said.

'I'll lift her out. Can you take her legs?'

Evie pulled the barouche alongside the car and nodded. Zac got his hands under Caroline's armpits and waited for a contraction to ease off. Evie squeezed in next to him, conscious of the heat radiating from his body. Zac started moving Caroline, pulling her out of the car. Evie reached for her legs, lifting her behind the knees and moving her onto the barouche. Together they whizzed Caroline into the hospital, Steve trailing behind them.

'OK, let's meet your baby. You can push with the next contraction,' Zac instructed Caroline once they were inside. 'That's it. Here comes the head. You're doing a great job. Rest for a minute, you'll need to push again when I tell you, to deliver the shoulders.' Zac's hands were ready to turn the baby's shoulders to guide it into the world. Evie felt a lump form in her throat at the sight of Zac waiting, ready to deliver a new life. He insisted a family wasn't an option for him but if he felt what she did, wouldn't he want to work through that?

Didn't he feel what she felt? She thought of their love-making. He'd felt the magic, that was one thing she didn't doubt.

'Now, Caroline, last push. Here we go.' There was a collective exhale as the tiny baby slid into Zac's waiting hands. 'You have a daughter, a perfect little girl.'

Evie was ready with the suction tubing and busied herself cleaning out the baby's airway. She couldn't bear to look at Zac. She could only imagine how difficult it must be to deliver other people's babies. Other people's daughters. Evie kept her focus on the newborn. She was tiny and wrinkled—being four weeks early, she hadn't had time to lay down fatty reserves. But Zac was right, she seemed perfect.

Evie stopped suctioning and the baby started to wail. Zac clamped and cut the cord. 'We need to warm your baby up, Caroline, while I deliver your placenta.' Evie hung the suction tube up, ready to take the baby, but as she turned around she was aware of another pair of hands waiting. Another nurse had arrived.

'I'm Susan,' she said, her voice cheery and reassuring. 'I've brought down a heat lamp and the humidicrib. There's a Vitamin K injection ready to go as well.' Susan took the baby in a warmed blanket, placing her under the heat lamp and running through the Apgar test. 'Seven out of ten,' she reported. 'Two point six one kilograms, thirty-four centimetres.'

'Your baby's fine, Caroline.' Zac kept talking as he delivered the placenta. Evie stood beside him as he checked it and Susan relayed information about the baby.

'Five minute Apgar score, nine out of ten.'

'Can I hold my baby now?' Caroline asked.

Zac nodded. 'Yes, of course.'

Susan brought the baby back to her parents. Evie stepped back and observed the new family. Caroline was on the bed, cuddling her daughter. Steve stood beside his wife, stroking her hair, a look of absolute amazement on his face. The baby nuzzled in, searching for her mother's breast.

Evie blinked back a tear. Newborn babies never failed to make her cry. She chanced a glance at Zac—how did he do this? She listened to him as he congratulated Caroline and Steve. He was saying all the right things but his expression was solemn.

It had to be hard. He congratulated the new family again and then turned away abruptly. The loss of his own daughter would be heavy in his heart but was he also thinking about his vow to lead a solitary life? It was obvious to her he wasn't made for that. He had love to give. Was he really going to deny himself that?

'Susan, let's take the family up to a maternity bed.' He gave Evie the briefest of acknowledgements before he left the department. 'Good result, everyone. Well done.'

And they were all gone, leaving Evie alone to clean up, Zac's heartache foremost on her mind.

She'd sell her soul if it would buy Zac peace.

The realisation she'd do anything for him, anything at all, stopped her in her tracks.

She was in love. In love with Zac.

She sank down onto a chair and tested the phrase again. It was true. She loved him.

When had it happened? She didn't know but there wasn't a doubt in her mind. She loved him with everything she had and she was going to fight for him. He was carrying a lot of pain, deep, raw pain, but there was still love to give, she knew it. Anyone who had loved before could love again. If he could move beyond the all-consuming belief that love hurt too much and promises were worthless.

How was she to convince him of that? To convince him to take a chance on her?

By the time she'd finished straightening up the

department, she knew how, or at least where to start. The first chance she got she was going to see Lexi.

Fate seemed to be on her side. Lexi had had a free appointment that same morning so she'd had her blood test, no questions asked and Lexi had promised to rush the results if she could.

It had been two days now, two days in which Evie had seen Zac only in passing. She'd acted as if everything was right with her world, letting him think he'd won her over with his arguments. He seemed preoccupied—but, then, he would be, with the nursing-home issue still hanging over his head.

Evie was at work when Lexi walked into the emergency department.

'What brings you here?'

Lexi had an envelope in her hand and she held it out to Evie as she spoke. 'Your results are back. I thought I'd bring them to you.'

Evie took the envelope. 'What do they say?'

'Don't you want to read them yourself?'

Evie hesitated, suddenly nervous despite her confidence it would be fine. 'No. You tell me.'

'You tested positive. You're a carrier.'

Surprise battled with disbelief. Disbelief won. 'There must be a mistake.' She couldn't be a carrier for CF.

She'd been assuming she'd be negative and she'd planned to use the results to convince Zac to give them a chance. But where did this result leave her now? It would be the final nail in the coffin of their relationship.

'They're definitely your results. I didn't ask before, but I can see it's upsetting news, so can I ask why you wanted to know? Does this have something to do with Zac's sister?'

'Can we treat this as part of the consult? Patient confidentiality and all that?'

'Of course.'

Revealing Zac's secrets about his marriage wasn't an option. Instead, she said, 'It is related to his sister. From what I can gather, Zac is terrified of having a child with CF and he won't get involved in case it gets serious.' An understatement if ever there was one, but how could she break Zac's confidence on the real reason for the break-up of the marriage? The termination of his baby's life behind his back.

'But you're already involved, aren't you?'

'I care for him, really care for him, like nothing

I've ever felt. And I was hoping, assuming really, I'd test negative and be able to lay his fears about taking a chance with me to rest. But it's not going to happen like that, is it?'

'I guess not but—' Lexi stopped in mid-sentence. 'Listen, it's Zac you need to talk to. If you care about him, you have to let him know. What have you got to lose?'

'My self-respect when he turns me down? Again?'

'If you care about him enough, I'd imagine that's a chance you'll take. Just like if he cares about you enough, he'll set aside his notions that he can't get involved just in case something bad happens. You've tested positive—big deal.' She emphasised her words with a shrug. But she didn't know the full story.

'There endeth the lesson?'

'Tom always says I go on too much but, that said, I'm here if you need to talk about this.'

'Thanks. I appreciate the offer.'

More talking would have to wait as a string of emergencies came through the door almost the moment Lexi left. A child with a nasty burn on his forearm after upending a cup of coffee over himself, a suspected case of meningitis that needed admission, a suspicious lump in a groin, which had been noticed weeks before but left until the pain had been excruciating, followed by a split chin from a fall in the bath.

But thinking didn't have to be postponed totally, and between the lump in the groin and the split chin, the solution presented itself.

If she was right—and maybe it was a big if—but if there was a chance he could feel the same way about her, then they wouldn't have children. That was the barrier between them.

They wouldn't have children.

Or they'd adopt.

She saw her last patient out and retreated to a cubicle to finish her thoughts between cases.

Why hadn't this occurred to her before? She'd been pouring out all her love to the children in the home in Vietnam, never thinking beyond it. She hadn't fallen in love before, not like this, so she'd never seriously thought about having children, had just assumed they were waiting somewhere in her future.

Of course they'd adopt.

It made perfect sense. Surely that's why fate had led her to Vietnam in the first place, to show her love didn't only come in one form.

They'd adopt from Vietnam if Australia had a programme established—hadn't she heard it was under negotiation? And if it wasn't, they'd adopt from another country they could both fall in love with, another country that could become a part of their life together. Vietnam had shown her the heart—her heart—didn't have a prescription for love. Love could be found in all sorts of places. The only thing that mattered was that when you found it, you celebrated it for the gift it was.

But how did she convince Zac that it was a gift, and not a curse?

CHAPTER NINE

'*CODE black. Code black. Medical staff to Emergency. Code Black.*'

Zac sprinted along the corridor, pulse racing, ready for any eventuality. But he wasn't prepared for the chaos that greeted him as he skidded into the emergency department.

There were bodies piled up in the middle of the floor, people yelling, orderlies running past him towards the writhing mass on the floor. It took him a few moments to comprehend the scene in front of him. It was difficult to tell where one person stopped and another started, but by the movement he assumed that most, if not all, were still breathing. There were two people in ambulance uniforms and another two in hospital uniforms all lying on top of a fifth person, who was yelling and thrashing about like a man possessed.

Zac stood, rooted to the spot, until one of the

ambos spied him and called out. 'Hey, Doc, come and give us a hand. This guy's gone crazy.'

Zac realised what was happening—they were trying to restrain the man at the bottom of the pile, who was having some kind of seizure. Zac moved, ready now to lend his weight to the effort. From the corner of his eye he saw Evie, tiny Evie, approaching the heaving pile. She held a syringe in her hand.

'Hold his arm,' she shouted.

Zac moved towards the man but one of the ambos moved faster, pinning the man's arm to the floor. But the change in his position had left one of the man's legs free, he kicked out, connecting with Evie and sending her crashing into a chair, her left arm taking the full force of her weight. Zac dived for the man's leg before he could do any more damage.

'Are you OK?'

Evie nodded as she picked herself up from the floor and came back to the patient. She still had hold of the syringe and this time she was able to get the needle into a vein. She depressed the plunger. 'Don't let him go.'

'What is that?' Zac asked.

'Midazolam. He's psychotic, another ice user.'

Evie emptied the contents of the syringe into

the patient and then disposed of the needle while the rest of them continued to pin the patient down, waiting for the sedative to take effect. She rubbed her upper arm, where she'd collided with the chair. Once the sedative took effect Evie issued instructions as a spinal board was assembled under the patient.

'He needs to go to ICU. He's had enough midazolam to stop a charging bull. They'll need to monitor him on an ECG and make sure his heart doesn't stop.'

The patient was lifted onto a barouche and wheeled to ICU, accompanied by one of the other nurses. Zac knew he should go but Evie was hurt. She was hugging her left arm against her body, rubbing it with her right hand.

'Let me look at that—you landed pretty heavily.'

'It's nothing,' she said, but she didn't resist when he led her to a cubicle and sat her in a chair. She looked exhausted and thinner than he remembered, even though it had only been a few days since he'd seen her properly.

He turned back the sleeve of her shirt, exposing the smooth, fair skin of her upper arm. Already there was a purple stain spreading across her skin. He ran his fingers lightly over the bruise and wasn't surprised to feel a large haematoma under the skin. Evie flinched at his touch, her face pale.

'I'm sorry, I know it hurts but I need to see what we're dealing with.'

'I'm OK.'

'Sure you are. Can you make a fist and bend your elbow?'

'Nothing's broken. It's just a knock,' she said, following his instructions. 'I'll put an ice-pack on it, it'll be fine.'

'And you? Are you OK?'

'A little the worse for wear.'

'Don't blame yourself. You weren't to know he'd kick out like that. If anyone's to blame, it's me. I was too slow off the mark.'

'I'm not talking about the patient, I'm talking about you and me.'

'Now isn't the time.'

'I have a feeling it's never the time, from your point of view. But I need to say this.' Her voice faltered a little. 'I care about you, Zac, and I can't pretend otherwise. I tried not to think about you, about us, but I couldn't do it. And then I thought I had the answer, I thought I'd be able to convince you to take a chance with me, so I asked Lexi for a blood test. I asked her to test for the CF gene.'

'Damn it, Evie. Why couldn't you just let it lie?' The wind had been knocked out of him. His legs gave way and he sat down heavily on the bed beside her chair.

'I couldn't because I can't live like that, ignoring the chance to have something wonderful. And I didn't promise you I would.'

'I've told you I can't get involved. You wanted to know why so I told you what I haven't told anyone other than my family. I did that because I thought you would understand. Can't you respect that?'

'I'm a carrier.' She blurted it out and he had a brief thought that this was not the way she'd planned on telling him before he really heard what she'd said.

She'd tested positive?

It didn't matter. It made no difference either way. 'Why can't you understand? Even if you weren't a carrier, we, you and I, couldn't go anywhere. I'm not getting involved.'

'So even if I was negative, you'd still be saying no?'

'Yes.'

'Does it make any difference if I tell you—?' She stopped and chewed at her bottom lip and he really, really didn't think he wanted to hear what she was about to say. 'I'm falling in love with you. I want to be with you. You. I don't care about getting pregnant, I don't need to have my own babies. I just want you.'

He was right. That was the one thing he didn't want to hear, the one thing above all others because, as much as he cared, he couldn't give her what she wanted. And he'd never meant it to end with pain for either of them, but of course pain was the one inevitable thing in life. Pain and death. He'd argue his way out of it, show her all the additional reasons why it could never be. He had to make her see sense.

'And Vietnam? London? Your work? Your life? The children waiting for you to return? What are you planning on doing about all that?'

'I'd give it all up if it means I can have you.'

'And children—you'd give up on having children, too?' He was incredulous. 'That's not a decision to make lightly.'

'I didn't say I didn't want children, I said I don't need to have biological children. We can adopt.'

She looked confident but had she given any thought to what she was announcing? As if she'd give up Vietnam! And not have children? Or adopt? Who came up with such life-changing ideas in a spilt second? Apparently Evie Henderson did. She rallied again, her confidence growing, and he didn't know what worried him most. 'None of it's as important as you.'

She was confused, she had to be confused to even think of suggesting such plans. Worst thing was, he knew how she felt, like the world had gone crazy. The difference was he knew enough to ignore it. You didn't change your path in life just because emotions swamped you when you weren't expecting it. Because it didn't last.

'Evie, we scarcely know each other.' His tone was harsh, angry, and he hated himself for it, but he had to make her understand, had to push her away, for her sake as much as his. He saw her blink back tears, fighting to control her emotions, but he was struggling to control his, too. Too many emotions were fighting for room inside his head. 'It's ludicrous to jump from discussing why we can't date to talking about options for a future together. We can't have this conversation. You decided to get tested despite me making it clear what my intentions were. We don't have a future.'

'You're telling me you won't give us a chance under any circumstances.'

'That's what I've consistently told you. And you say you'd stay, say you won't bear children, but they're spur-of-the-moment decisions, promises even, you'd never keep.' He held up a hand to silence her objection. 'You think you will now, but that'll change.'

'You think you know what I want more than I do?' Her voice was quieter now. Angry or hurt? He thought of what he'd just said to her and knew it was both, but he had to make her understand.

'I know promises made with the best of intentions are still liable to be broken.'

'You know me so well? I know you, too. And you care for me, too, I know it. When we ma—' She broke off, flustered, and waved her hand instead. 'The other night, I saw it, felt it. You cared. I've never begged someone to be with me. So if the truth is you don't like me enough to be with me, even short term, just tell me.'

'It was only ever a fling.' How could he do this to her? 'We both knew that.' How could he not?

'It was more than that, and you know it.' Two red blotches appeared on her cheeks as she vented her anger at him. 'So tell me straight, what's the real story? I'm not good enough? No one is ever going to be good enough?'

'Maybe you're right.' The pain it cost him to say those words very nearly tipped him over the edge, very nearly had him pulling her to him, kissing away all the hurt and confusion and promising her the world. But he'd only break that promise later, tomorrow or next month—it made no difference—but break it he would. One of them would. It was better to have the pain now.

She looked close to tears. Frustration, disbelief and anguish were burning behind those dark eyes, which were impossibly liquid in their expressiveness. He'd be tortured for nights at the look of bewildered hurt he saw before she turned away, before she turned her back on him. Now it was only her narrow shoulders peeking through a tumble of dark curls—curls he'd tangled his fingers in only days ago, lost in the exquisite rapture of her—he could see.

He didn't know how to respond—he couldn't undo the hurt, he couldn't offer what she wanted. So he stayed quiet. An option he should have exercised earlier.

She'd raised her head now but still faced away from him and, heel that he knew himself to be, he was glad because he didn't have to confront the accusation of betrayal he knew was still burning brightly in her eyes. 'If that's what it really is, that I'm not good enough to make you risk feeling again, loving again, then...then...' She stopped, took a great gulp of air and said, 'Then you deserve to be alone.'

She stood up from the chair in one smooth movement, threw back her shoulders, tossed her head and stalked to the door. Her hand on the handle, she turned around to add, 'Just so there's no doubt, we're over. For good.'

If it were only a matter of him believing she wasn't good enough, he thought as he left the hospital, then he would deserve to be alone, just as she'd said. Very alone. For ever.

He'd left her thinking she wasn't good enough.

In three years, he hadn't been tempted to spend an hour with a woman other than as friends. Then Evie had come along and he'd fallen under her spell at lightning speed, so fast he hadn't even known it had been happening until he'd pulled her into his arms that first time and kissed her as if life itself depended on it. Then they'd made love and the world had shifted. And the shock of what they'd discovered together finally kicked a desperate self-preservation into gear, shattering the illusion he'd allowed to shroud their time together. Shattered it into a thousand pieces and held a nightmarish mirror up to his eyes to remind him of what loss felt like.

How had he forgotten, even for a second? But he had, and now he'd caused them both pain and a new cruel ache had lodged in his heart. He hadn't thought there was room for more pain but he hadn't even touched the surface. But if he didn't end it now, there'd be worse to come later.

So he had no choice.

She wasn't thinking straight. He'd give anything to throw himself into that heady senselessness with her, but one of them had to think for both of them.

Because she'd never stay.

And he'd never give himself like she deserved. He'd never be free of ties to the past, free to love her as she wanted.

He couldn't love like that.

He didn't do love and he didn't do tears, not since his daughter.

It didn't matter about the genetics. It didn't matter if they could or couldn't have children together.

What mattered was that he was never putting himself in the way of the pain that had ripped him apart when his child had died.

And letting Evie convince him with her passion and her crazy plans for having a life together would only ever end in pain. He'd just proved that point.

She'd promised she'd stay, promised she didn't care about being pregnant. Sooner or later, her promises would crumble and turn to dust. He was certain of that.

His wife had made similar promises in good faith. She'd vowed to love him for ever, sworn it wouldn't matter if their child had CF. She hadn't been a bad person, quite the contrary. But she'd broken her promises just the same.

And he didn't blame her. For all the promises in the world, no one ever knew how they'd react when life played one of her cruel tricks.

Which was why he didn't do love.

And why he'd rather break both their hearts now. Because if it was inevitable, he'd rather get it over with. Better than waiting until she became

so much a part of his life that having it end would
hurt more than he could bear.

Evie returned to work despite her bruised and
aching arm but spent every moment praying to
whichever gods were listening for a miracle, to
wind back the clock and erase the last hours from
her life. Give her another version. Give her Zac.

The girls were going to a friend's house for the
night, straight from school, so she was free—but
it was the last thing she wanted. It meant having
time to deal with what had just happened.

What had just happened was that her heart had
been ripped from her chest. Her earlier concern
that her pride would be bruised didn't even rate
a mention compared to the pain of being rejected
in no uncertain terms. She'd never thought it
would really happen like that.

But it had.

And worst of all, Zac had been trying to extri-
cate himself from her right from the start. She'd
read it all wrong and made an idiot of herself in
the process. Had she really just told him she
didn't care if they didn't have children, that she'd
stay here and give up her life, her dreams, her
passions? Heat flooded her face and she could

scarcely stand to stay in her skin, so acute was the humiliation pumping through her. She'd thrown herself at him, made all sorts of rash promises—and he didn't want her! She needed to run and run and escape until she'd left only her shadow behind to deal with the mortification. But it didn't work that way.

There was nothing but time to ease the wrenching anguish slicing through her chest, carving her in two.

So by the time her shift ended, she was intent on fuelling her anger so she didn't have to feel the pain.

Distraction and denial were great strategies—how long could she rely on them?

For ever?

She dawdled when it eventually came time to go, hoping for divine intervention to keep her at the hospital. Her prayers were answered. A message came from Pam, asking her to go to the nursing-home.

Fundraising business, she thought. Just what she needed to keep her busy. She made it there in record time and the common room was buzzing with excitement when she entered.

She saw Pam and headed over.

'Evie! Fantastic news!' Pam's face was glowing with excitement, oblivious to Evie's strained demeanour. 'The government isn't going to cut the funding. The nursing-home won't be closed.'

'That's fantastic. When did you hear?' Her voice sounded tinny and forced even though this was what she'd been praying for. Distraction. She seized it, not just with both hands but with every molecule in her body.

'The CEO announced it after a board meeting ten minutes ago, then we got a call from that nice Victoria Knapman—she was so excited for us.'

Ms Knapman's excitement probably had more to do with the positive media coverage she'd receive, but Evie kept her own counsel.

'The CEO was going to tell you but as we have you to thank for this in large part, I asked if I could speak to you first so you could share the news with the residents.'

What would Zac think about her being credited like this? 'That's very kind but my part would have been minimal. The board has done the hard yards and I think Fel and Nancy might have had major roles, being the media's sweethearts.'

Pam didn't look convinced but let the subject

slide. 'The residents have been asking if the fair will still go ahead. It would be a shame to cancel it, everyone's worked so hard.'

She was right, the fair was no longer necessary for financial or publicity reasons. But it had done so much to occupy the time and minds of the residents, how could they cancel it?

And she needed it as much as the residents. Distraction, distraction, distraction. She'd deal with her rejection and her pain later.

Like next year.

Next year, when she'd finally made it back to Vietnam and could make a new start. Next year, when she was back where what she had to give meant something, where she could cuddle and kiss love into the hearts of children, nurture them, teach them to trust again when life had been so hard and cruel. She wasn't what Zac wanted so she'd go where she was wanted, where she was needed. She was good enough and she wouldn't be told otherwise.

She'd deal with the raw pain inside her later and until that time she'd pretend it didn't exist. Maybe it would go away all by itself if she pretended hard enough.

'Of course we'll go ahead with the fair,' she

said, her voice full of confidence. Pretending like a professional already.

'I told you she'd forge ahead, Nancy.' Evie heard Fel's voice behind her.

'Thank goodness, or we'll be resting our coffee-cups on mounds of calendars for years to come.'

'What calendars?' she asked.

'These.' Fel held up a calendar with tear-off pages, one per month, and to cries of '*Playboy, eat your heart out*' and 'Ta da!' the cover was flipped over to reveal a black and white photograph of a beach on which half a dozen naked 'elderly citizens' were walking off into the sunset on their walking sticks and walking frames, the assorted shapes and sizes of their backsides forming a glorious central focus for the photo.

'Oh, my!' Evie started laughing, despite herself. 'You didn't?'

'We most certainly did. If it's good enough for those English women, it's good enough for us.' Fel's eyes sparkled green with mischief. 'Can you pick who is who? Mind, there's been no digital enhancement, so we can take full credit for our beauty.'

'I think I can.' Evie bent to take a closer look.

'Tell me you didn't both adorn your backsides with tattoos for this?'

'Unfortunately they're only temporary,' said Nancy. 'And all the store had was skulls or roses.'

'The tattoo parlour won't touch you if you're the wrong side of seventy,' added Fel, her voice filled with exaggerated offence.

Evie peered closer. 'So you went with the skulls option. Charming.' She shook her head at them. If she pretended hard enough, maybe the pretence that everything was right with her world would work its magic and become real. Fat chance.

'Zac won't like it one little bit,' said Fel, with no small measure of satisfaction.

Had Fel looked closely at her again as she'd said that? Evie kept her face impassive and changed the topic. She couldn't go there. Too raw, too painful, too humiliating. 'How did you manage to get the calendar done so quickly?'

'Digital technology,' said Fel. 'Shuffling about naked on the beach was easy, we were only nervous about being stuck with the stock if the fair was cancelled.'

'Then you'd be left sweet-talking the current affairs crew into buying them,' said Nancy to Fel and Evie.

'You know they won't be back now the nursing-home story is no longer news?' Evie said.

'I hadn't thought that far,' said Fel.

'I'll buy one for everyone I know if I need to, but the fair is on and I suspect you'll sell out in an hour.'

'Zac's made the same promise.'

Zac and promises were not what she wanted to talk about. She made a show of checking her watch. 'Is that the time? I have to run. I've got people to see if this fair is going to be a success.'

Her attempt to deflect Fel's question failed. 'Have you two had a falling-out?'

Evie shrugged in response.

'Don't let what is meant to be slip away without a fight.'

Did Fel know what had happened? 'Sometimes our fate is in our hands. Other times, it's not. I'm learning to know the difference.'

It was just a pity she hadn't worked it out before she'd made such a spectacular fool of herself.

Evie was used to being surrounded by people at work but she'd always been content with her own company, too. Probably a result of the years she spent battling chronic fatigue syndrome. But since her fallout with Zac she found herself longing for a friendly face and a warm hug so it was with great relief she prepared to welcome Letita home. She pushed open the hospital door, eager to see her sister-in-law and find out how she'd survived the transfer back to Pelican Beach Hospital. She wasn't greeted with the enthusiasm she'd expected.

'Evie! You look terrible.'

'Thanks very much. You're the one recovering from major surgery, not me.'

'I know, which makes it even worse. What's happened?'

'Nothing's happened.'

Letitia fixed Evie with a hard stare. Evie sighed and elaborated. 'OK. To be more precise, nothing I want has happened. Zac has told me, in no uncertain terms, he doesn't want me.' She filled Letitia in on the details, pretending it didn't hurt half as much as it did. She'd been pinning her hopes on the pretence-become-reality wish for hour upon hour now. Wishes came true sometimes, didn't they? 'End result is, he told me point blank the real reason we couldn't be together was because he doesn't care about me like that.' She blinked away memories. Too much painful detail. 'He'd been trying to let me down gently, I guess, until I made that impossible. At the end of the day, the question of children aside, I'm not the woman he wants.'

'Why did he get involved with you in the first place if he didn't like you?'

'Seven-year itch? Or, in his case, the three-year itch. Convenience? Opportunity? It doesn't matter why, the problem is I'm not good enough to change his mind. Maybe if the right woman came along and blew rationality out of the water, hauled him beyond his safety net of detachment, he'd have to take the chance. But I'm not that woman.'

'And now?'

'Now I have a plan and I intend to stick to it.'

'A plan?'

'I'm going back to Vietnam. I was thinking I'd start over when I got back there, thinking that was going to be a long time to wait, and then I realised I didn't have to wait.'

'Just like that?'

Why were people always saying that to her? What other way was there to make decisions?

Letitia hadn't finished. 'You're leaving? Just when your mum is coming?'

Evie's parents had called the previous night to confirm the business had been sold and her mother would be arriving soon, leaving her father to make the final arrangements. Her mum would be here for Jake and the girls. She'd spoken to HR and had been assured they could, miraculously enough, replace her quite easily. She could go.

'How can I stay? I have to preserve some measure of self-respect. I need to go back to where what I do matters.' Taking a steadying breath, she said, 'I'm going to miss you all like crazy, especially the girls, but I need to do this. I'm going where I can make a difference.'

Letitia thought it over. 'But how will you afford that? You've always worked in the UK to support your time in Vietnam.'

'I'm hazy on the details, but it'll sort itself out. With the astoundingly huge exception of Zac, fate usually sets things straight.'

'I couldn't live like that, not planning, not knowing.'

'You live by your heart, Letitita, you do what feels right inside. That's all I do, too, it's just that what's right for you isn't right for me. I thought briefly it might be, settling down and all the rest, but I've been left in no doubt that's not the case.

I have other things I need to be doing. So I am.' Her smile was wry, but at least after their chat she could smile again. 'Broken heart and all.'

She stood and leant to kiss Letitia goodbye.

'You won't talk—?'

Evie held up a hand to silence her plea. 'I have my limits when it comes to being rejected. I made a mistake, Letitia. He's not the man I thought I was falling for. I thought he cared. I'm not saying he's horrible, I'm saying he read me wrong and that's my fault, in part. He tried to let me down gently and I was too distracted by attraction to take the hint.'

Leaving Letitia, she headed for the foreshore, to walk through the area that by tomorrow night would be a hive of activity as those involved in the fair arrived to set up for the next day. Her heart was heavy in her chest as she passed the bench where she'd sat with Zac. The bench where he'd kissed her.

She'd walk, and she'd think, and she'd plan. People kept saying, 'Just like that?' when she spoke of her plans. What they didn't know was that she did think things through, she just didn't fight her gut instinct about things, she went with her intuition and that was nearly always the right way to go. Nearly. Except, as she'd told her sister-in-law, with the momentous exception of Zac.

She might be spontaneous, she might know how to silence a room with a twist of her hips, and people might judge her for that, but she wasn't stupid. Displaying the raw pain she felt inside was not an option. Neither was sticking around, hoping Zac would change his mind.

She was done with begging.

She was through with humiliation.

Whatever Zac and she had shared had been a fiction.

And waiting around for him to realise he'd written a dud ending wasn't going to happen.

Two more days—three at the most—and she'd be in Vietnam with the people who had stolen her heart a long time before Zac Carlisle had come into her life.

People who didn't doubt she was worth something, who knew she had something to offer.

Children who needed her.

And if the children's home would have her, if she could find some way of making a living while she volunteered there, if she was lucky, the move would be permanent.

* * *

It took all of thirty minutes for the news to reach Zac.

Evie was leaving.

HR had already given her the OK to go. With all her support for the fair, it seemed people were happy to do her favours. And she was happy to take them.

How long had her resolve to stay lasted? A blink in time and she'd changed her mind.

He dismissed the thought she was leaving because he'd made it impossible for her to stay. Her family was here. Apparently her mother, who she hadn't seen in well over two years, was arriving any day. If love and family meant so much to her, she'd be staying. She'd promised to look after her nieces. She was bailing out at the first opportunity.

Love and family didn't mean so much after all.

She was just like everyone else. A promise was a promise only as long as it suited. After that, it was just an inconvenience to be circumvented as imaginatively as possible.

Taking the first plane out of the country was one way.

And if he'd let himself believe her promises,

she'd be taking his heart with her, too. Thank goodness he'd resisted. At least this way his heart was intact.

Just.

CHAPTER TEN

'GRANNY!'

'She's here, she's here!'

From their vantage point at the front window, Gracie and Mack's squeals announced Jake's arrival from the Adelaide airport with their grand-mother.

Evie raced up the passage, opened the door and narrowly avoided being bowled over by her nieces, who were beside themselves with excitement.

'You've got so big, Gracie!' June wrapped her granddaughters in arms that were always ready to hug. 'You're almost as tall as Auntie Evie, Mack. Evie, have you been eating? There's nothing of you.'

'Come in and give me a proper hello before you start nagging me, Mum.' Evie, stepped into her mum's arms, biting back tears that were always ready to fall, no matter how old she was, when life wasn't going well, and June gave her a hug. Blinking hard, she covered up her distress. 'I have to head over to the fairground in a moment to help set up. If you're not too tired, you should come with me.'

'I'm a retiree now, honey. I've got energy for everything.'

So twenty minutes later all five of them left for the fairground, although what contribution the little ones would make, Evie wasn't sure.

The fairground, set up on the wide strip of grass along the foreshore, was already looking festive, dotted with hired tents and trailers and an odd assortment of other, more makeshift shelters. The old Ferris wheel had been garlanded with lights, the organising committee had booked a jumping castle, rock-climbing wall and mini-golf, the food stalls were decked out with signs advertising their wares and a stage for entertainment was being erected. People hurried to and fro and the atmosphere was already one of excitement as they prepared for the next day's fair.

'A Shetland pony ride!' Mack and Gracie saw the sign and dragged Jake off to find the ponies.

'They'll be looking for a while. I doubt the ponies will be here before tomorrow,' Evie commented.

'What can I do to help?' June asked.

'Let's go to the Country Women's Association tent and see if they can do with a hand. I know most of the people there, they've been feeding us while Jake's been away.'

Within minutes June had been welcomed into the fold like a long-lost sister and, with her sleeves rolled up, was busy folding serviettes and arranging tables ready for the Devonshire teas the CWA would be serving.

'You're in your element, Mum. You're going to love living here.'

'I can't wait to have a social life and people to help now we're out of the truck stop.'

Evie had a light-bulb moment—was there one more thing she could put into place before she left? 'If being busy and meeting lots of people is what you want, I might have something just perfect for you. You'll have to give me a few hours to mull it over.'

'You and your dreaming, Evie. You've always had something going on, even as a child.' June gave her a kiss and resumed the conversation she'd been having with Mrs Lees about flourless chocolate cake, working all the while. Her mother was made for the CWA, for living in a community where people got involved and helped one another. Her mother was made to live in Pelican Beach among people like Mrs Lees and Fel and Nancy.

Leaving the tent, Evie spied Greg Evans, the CEO of the hospital, being shown the PA system on the stage, ready to open the fair tomorrow with the mayor. Just the man she wanted. Providence was letting her know her plan had been approved. He saw her when he left the stage and came straight over, pumping her hand with gratitude.

'This is due to you, Evie, and although there were various reasons why the government back-tracked, the pressure you put on them by showing the community was committed and ready to fight played its part. Thank you.'

'It was my pleasure.' He'd thanked her before, she didn't need more thanks. It wasn't why she'd got involved.

'Isn't there anything we can do to persuade you to stay? You've breathed new life into the nursing-home, it's a shame to see you go.'

'That's what I wanted to talk to you about. I can't stay but I have an idea. Do you have a few minutes?'

They bent their heads together and Evie gave him her pitch, the best she could manage given the idea had occurred to her less than ten minutes ago. Zac would never jump in like this, she thought as she spoke with enthusiasm to cover the rough patches in her plans.

Not that she cared two hoots what Zac would and wouldn't do.

But, she deliberated, as she looked at the stage and thought of one of the planned events, there was one more parting gift she could give Pelican Beach. One she didn't need the CEO's approval for.

'I can't believe I'm doing this,' Zac muttered to himself as he stood in the stall selling calendars emblazoned with photos of his naked, elderly aunt. Hundreds of people were browsing through the stalls in the warm summer sunshine or sitting on the grass in front of the stage, watching a succession of local performers, some excellent, some woeful. The smell of hot dogs and hot chips wafted on the air. None of it was putting him in the festive mood.

'Relax and enjoy. You're now an official accomplice in our dark deeds,' said Fel as she took money from an older gentleman in the queue and handed him his calendar. He winked at her and held out his calendar for her to sign.

'Which one are you?' the customer asked Zac.

Zac forced a smile. 'They knocked me back. I wasn't centrefold material.'

'No, but you're bachelor-of-the-year material,' said a lady in the line. 'My money's on you. For my daughter,' she added, when her friend nudged her in the ribs.

Zac handed her a calendar—what on earth was she talking about?

The fair had been officially opened by the mayor, who was now introducing Greg. Zac turned to the next customer while he listened with half an ear to the CEO.

He should have paid more attention. Before he knew it, he heard his name called and the line of people in front of the calendar stall became a swarm with the express purpose of propelling him onto the stage before he could refuse. Perhaps he'd resisted, but he was taken by surprise and then there he was, looking out at the crowd, which had now swelled to ridiculous numbers, standing in line with another five or six bewildered locals about his age. The butcher, the owner of the news agency, the local radio announcer, a high-school teacher and a dairy farmer. The only thing they had in common, as far as he could work out, was—

'Oh, no,' he groaned. They were all single.

'Oh, yes, they're doing things the traditional country way,' said the butcher, 'and having a beauty contest.'

'And we're the judges?'

That drew a wry laugh. 'The contestants.'

He glanced left and right—what were his chances of making a run for it?

'Don't even think of it. I've got first dibs on a quick escape and I'll tackle you for it.' Paul the butcher, laughed. 'Come on, mate, relax. Get into the spirit.'

What spirit? Did grumpy old men have spirit? That's how he was feeling. Grumpy. Old. Miserable.

Greg was hamming it up in his introduction, most of which Zac had now missed, so he had no idea what was happening when six women came onto the stage and deposited cooking utensils on a table.

Evie.

The world stopped.

Evie was one of the women.

The women approached the men and led them to the tables set out with bowls and eggs and egg beaters.

Evie smiled as though she didn't have a care in the world. She also didn't seem to have a thought for him, refusing eye contact with him and making straight for Paul, taking him by the arm. Anyone would think Paul had just won a sausage-stuffing competition he was grinning so much, but what man wouldn't be happy to have Evie standing slap-bang in front of him, in cut-off denim shorts and a brightly patterned vest top, hair loose, dark eyes shining? Dark eyes that weren't looking in his direction.

'Egg beaters at the ready. First one to crack six eggs, separate them, beat the whites and hold the bowl upside down over their heads without any spillage, is the winner of this round. Automatic elimination for the last to finish.'

If he finished last, he'd get out of there.

If he finished last, he'd lose in front of Evie.

The whistle blew and Zac had his first egg cracked and in the bowl while the butcher was still making eyes at Evie. He wasn't a doctor for nothing. If it was concentration he needed, that was what he had. Six egg whites were in the bowl and he was beating the white liquid into frothy peaks. The news-agency guy was one step ahead, lifting his bowl—could he overtake him? He assessed the eggs. No, not quite there. A few more flicks of the wrist... The crowd roared with laughter and clapped and Zac took a quick look to see the news agent's head covered in still runny egg whites—too quick off the mark.

He was done. He lifted his bowl, said a quick prayer and held it upside down over his head. The crowd roared—and the eggs stayed put.

Zac spun his bowl back down as the next contestant, then the next, held bowls aloft with varying degrees of success.

Paul came last. 'Deliberate, buddy. The early bird catches the worm and I'm going to introduce myself to the little lady.'

Zac's stomach muscles clenched and they both turned to find Evie but she was already in deep conversation with contestant number two who'd been hot on Zac's heels. Had she even seen him win?

Now there were five bachelors left. Pie-eating came next, after which Evie disappeared—with Paul? Zac was so distracted by that thought he made a mess of the knit-a-line competition and only just managed to scrape through. He blitzed the fillet-a-fish task, thankful the butcher had gone before that one. That left two of them—him and the news-agency guy, Tony.

Then he heard it.

Arabic music.

He closed his eyes and prayed, hoping it wouldn't mean what he thought.

The gods weren't listening.

Greg announced the competition and the crowd roared their approval just as Zac's world froze at the news. A dance-off. What was Greg saying? The last task was to have been a sleeping-bag race around the stage, but a late offer from Pelican Beach's most eligible woman had upped the stakes. Evie would teach the two finalists how to shimmy and shake, and the loudest applause from the crowd would decide the winner.

As Evie ran lightly onto the stage, the crowd went wild.

Clothed in a bright pink skirt that swished around her calves and sat low on her hips—those hips!—a heavily beaded bra top, showing every enticing curve, her eyes highlighted with dark eyeliner, her cheeks flushed, she took her place in the centre of the stage, rousing the crowd to join in, apparently enjoying the catcalls and whistles and clapping.

If he'd humiliated her with his rejection, he knew he was about to pay for it now.

He resigned himself to the fate he deserved.

She was in front of them, giving them instructions, laughing as his competition, Tony, made a joke.

'Are you ready, boys?' Even her voice was in character, every part of her the seductress. She could have been his. For a while, she could have been his. But it would never have been for ever.

Did for ever matter?

He thought of his baby, the one he'd never know, and thought of the pain that remained in his heart still. Pain that would be with him for ever. For ever did matter.

'Ready,' said Tony, earning himself a gorgeous smile from Evie.

If for ever mattered, then the opinion Evie would take with her of him mattered, too.

He sought her eyes, finding a blank gaze. No smile for him.

'I take no prisoners,' was all she said, adding a

teasing smile for Tony's benefit. The smile died on her lips as his eyes met hers. He knew her words had been a challenge to him.

He'd match it, rise to the occasion. 'Ready,' he announced, giving his hips a half-decent twist, to thunderous applause from the crowd.

That earned him his first smile from Evie, but it was thin. It said she'd match his challenge.

And they were off.

First, learning to bend from the knees, not the hips, the secret of belly dancing. The crowd joined in the tempo of the music kicked up a notch, the beat irresistible. She was irresistible. The movements came thick and fast, rocking the hips, lifting the hips, shimmying the arms, twisting the wrists. Men's wrists weren't made to bend like that! His hips weren't separate from his torso! But he'd bend and twist and rock and shimmy if it did him permanent injury. He had no doubt he'd never looked so ridiculous but at least there were two of them—and the crowd was coming along for the ride, too.

And the one thing he knew was he wasn't quitting, even if his hips never moved again. But Tony wasn't quitting either.

The music ended and the crowd cheered. Their

laughter and applause was deafening, and they cheered louder when Greg came on stage to thank Evie before announcing that Pelican Beach's most eligible bachelor was, by a whisker, Tony the news agent.

It was over. He'd gone along with it in the spirit of the fair and had come second. As he left the stage, he reminded himself he was happy not to have won—Tony would be fielding offers from women all day now, even if only in jest, and he didn't want to deal with that.

What he wanted was to find Evie.

She was leaving Pelican Beach. He had to try and put things straight. She'd be coming back to visit her family and he needed to make sure they could be civil when she did. That was why he needed to see her. It had nothing to do with the feelings she'd roused in him when he'd seen her on stage, watched her dance, seen the life and joy in her face as she'd moved. The shadows in her eyes when she'd first appeared on stage had disappeared as she'd danced, oblivious to her audience, at one with the beat and the rhythm of the music, in her own world, where everything was magic.

It had nothing to do with feeling his heart expand with bitter-sweet joy as he'd watched her, combined with the pain of knowing she was leaving.

It had nothing at all to do with how he felt. He only needed to make amends in some small way.

He was just doing the right thing. Again.

So why did the right thing leave him feeling so damn rotten?

He found her by the Ferris wheel, talking with Tony and Paul, laughing with them. He put his question to her. 'I hate to interrupt, but could I speak to you for a moment? It's about the hospital.'

Medicine was never questioned as an excuse. The other men left them to it but not before promising to seek her out later.

'You don't need me for work. I'm not on call and neither are you.'

She'd changed her clothes now, no longer the dancing gypsy, but her eyes were still highlighted with dark liner, her cheeks still flushed, her hair tumbling down over her shoulders. She was still lovely. And still as little disposed to be near him, judging by the distant expression in her eyes.

'No, but I wanted to talk to you. I heard you're leaving.'

She looked away, didn't confirm or deny, just looked away. Then she said, a bite in her voice,

'And it took seeing other men being interested to make you care about that?'

'That's not why I'm here, but I can accept you might think that.'

The Ferris wheel came to a halt and the people shuffled off. 'Ride with me?' He put out a hand to take hers but she shrugged it away. Still, she joined the line and waited while a cage was opened for them, sitting herself as far over to her side as she could manage.

'Evie, there are things I need to say before you go. I know I've hurt you, and I'm sorry. It was never my intention.'

She shrugged and looked out over the fairground, away from him.

He opened his mouth to apologise again but instead asked the question that had been on his mind ever since he'd heard her news. 'Why are you leaving? Your mum has just arrived back, you haven't seen your dad yet, and Letitia is still in hospital.'

He had to know whether her promises to stay, to make a life together, had amounted to nothing, or whether there was some all-compelling reason she had to leave. He had no right, but he couldn't restrain himself.

She turned to face him, anger blazing in her eyes. 'You're seriously asking me to explain myself?'

'You said you'd stay if we were together. You were offended when I said I thought you'd leave one day.'

'I would have stayed for you. But you're not asking me to.' She was angry and agitated and hurt, clearly hurt. 'Are you?'

The Ferris wheel jerked to a halt, their cage swinging mid-air, suspended in no-man's-land. Just like him. She was waiting for his answer. He couldn't give her the one she wanted.

'I never meant to hurt you but I couldn't start something I know has to end.'

'Really?' Her tone was dry but he could feel the fury underneath it. The Ferris wheel creaked to a start again and she grabbed at the side rail. 'The way I see it, you already did.'

She was right. He had. She had every reason to despise him and from the way she was glaring at him now, it seemed she'd thought of them all.

The cage swung down towards the ground— they'd almost completed one revolution. He'd brought her here to let her know he was sorry, but somehow he'd managed to imply she'd lied to him and she'd never have stayed anyway. He'd made her hate him in the time it had taken to complete one full circle on the Ferris wheel.

Their cage reached the ground and the wheel slowed down but didn't stop. Evie pulled the pin and unlocked the door, scrambling out while the wheel continued to turn. She stumbled in the process but Tony was waiting there for her and scooped her up, half lifting her away from the wheel.

The wheel rose again, leaving him to watch as the woman he'd managed to drive away was held close to the chest of another man. Pelican Beach's most eligible bachelor no less.

They disappeared from sight.

The wheel rose higher as his heart plummeted in the opposite direction.

CHAPTER ELEVEN

To: Evie@emailme.com
From: letitiaandjake@pelicanmail.com.au
Subject: the coffee might be good but so is an email once in a while
We haven't heard from you for weeks (at least three). What's news in Ho Chi Minh City? Thanks to your sweet-talking of the CEO, your mum is having a ball organising fundraising and social events in the nursing-home as the new Activities Queen—she's even on the payroll—and your dad is now busy fixing things around the hospital (he's not yet on the payroll, I'll keep you posted. What is it with your family and helping out?). On another note, you won't ask so I'm telling you, Zac looks like he's been told he's got three weeks to live, i.e. not great. He restrains himself to only ask after you in a polite way but I can see

he's aching to know every little thing. I know he hurt you but are you sure there's no hope? Won't stick my oar in any more. We love you, stay safe and drop us a line.

To: letitiaandjake@pelicanmail.com.au
From:Evie@emailme.com
Subject: all is well…
But email access is not easy, hence lack of them. I'm working in the medical care pro-gramme with children up to age eighteen, heart-breaking but uplifting. One little guy, Tran (but he prefers Jonno) has stolen my heart. He is HIV positive, abandoned by his family, too poor to provide for him. Don't know what the future holds, we're doing all we can. My dream is to spend a few months at least in the foundation's rural medical station in Mekong Delta if the anti-malarials hold out. Please don't tell me about Zac, it's too hard to hear since there is no hope. I'm still hurt beyond words but the truth is, if there was a way I could have been a bigger fool, I can't think of it. Pray for Jonno. Love you, miss you all, Evie

* * *

To: Evie@emailme.com
From: letitiaandjake@pelicanmail.com.au
Subject: Good news!!
I coaxed your anti-technology mum into looking at the website for where you are and she's now knee-deep in raising the funds to give you your three months at the rural centre and sponsor a child—we're hoping it will be Jonno. Will keep you posted, but I now know where you get your 'can do' attitude! Pelican Beach is right behind her (so is Zac—you wouldn't believe how he's thrown himself into the project). Love L

To: letitaandjake@pelicanmail.com.au
From: Evie@emailme.com
Jonno died two days ago. Very sudden. He got pneumonia and his immune system just collapsed. Six days ago I told you he was doing well, and he was. Now his wasted little body is all that's left. Is there anything after death? How can I not believe that a child's spirit lives on, even if it's only in our love for them? Pray for him. We bury him tomorrow. This is where I'm

meant to be for now, and I know one day there will be another child who is meant to have me for a mother. Love hurts but I'm going to keep on doing it. Love to all of you, Evie.

'Letitia, you're in danger of becoming permanently attached to that thing.' Zac entered Letitia's hospital room and waved a hand at her laptop, lying, where it always was, on her lap in her bed.

'It's amazing how addictive the internet is and, of course, I never know when I'm going to hear from Evie.' She pursed her lips and considered him for a moment, her blue eyes thoughtful. 'Which I just have. I know you never ask to read her emails but I'm also pretty sure I'm getting a few more visits from you than is strictly necessary just in case I have any news. I told you about the little boy, Jonno?'

He nodded. He'd had recurring visions of Evie with a dark-haired child, holding him, laughing with him, showing him someone cared. Showing him he was loved.

'But this one,' Letitia went on, 'I think you should read for yourself.'

He hesitated—was that trespassing? But Letitia hadn't offered before so she must have thought it through. It was only because of Letitia that he knew anything about Evie's life in the last two months. He knew what he was doing, knew where his future lay, but hearing about her let him feel it was possible she'd be part of his life again one day.

He took the laptop and read. It was like hearing her voice again. She wrote the way she spoke and the emotion rang out in her words.

Jonno had died? The email was dated yesterday—was she burying him now, while he read? He gritted his teeth and swore under his breath. He should have been with her, should have moved things along more quickly—but there were things to do. He had to get it right if he had any chance of setting things straight with her.

'I can see you still care, Zac, despite what you told her.'

He handed the laptop back to her, not trusting himself to meet her eyes without losing control. 'I do still care. I just didn't realise how much until I'd made a complete hash of it all and she'd gone.'

'I'll only say one thing, then. Don't let too

much time pass by if you intend to set things straight.'

He'd held himself back. He'd needed to know he was doing the right thing. He didn't want to act on a whim and end up hurting them both even more. But Letitia was right. He hoped he hadn't left it too late.

The noise and chaos was unbelievable. Even from the vantage point of the taxi window, wound down to let some breeze in to combat the stifling humidity, it was hard to take in. The smells of the street stalls and the fumes from the traffic, the roar of vehicles, the multitude of sights, the mass of people, the stalls and shops, the architecture, all so unfamiliar, combined to assault his senses.

Mopeds and motorbikes packed the roads, the drivers appearing oblivious to the need to stick to one side of the road, weaving around other vehicles at crazy angles, multiple passengers piled up on the bike more often than not. He'd counted three children, two adults and a large basket of shopping on one—how did they stay on? But they did. The road was large enough for two lanes in each direction, but the drivers seemed to have decided at least seven lanes would be better and used the road accordingly.

Car horns honked, and among it all pedestrians simply walked out onto the roads, apparently trusting the traffic would swerve around them. It was like nothing Zac had ever seen before but it seemed to work.

His taxi cut across the path of a van, a truck and a motorbike, pulled sharply round a corner into a side street and screeched to a halt in front of a long, low brick building. He wasn't a religious man but he'd been dishing up prayers for most of the trip. The driver turned around and beamed at him, waiting for payment for a job well done. Was it? Zac peered out the window and spotted a large brass sign, lettered in black, announcing this was, indeed, the foundation. Counting out the unfamiliar notes until he reached the price they'd agreed on, he added a bit extra to thank the gods he'd made it there in one piece. The driver nodded his head fervently and insisted on helping Zac get his luggage out of the boot.

And then he was alone, on the doorstep, the chaos of the main street receding in the distance, the foundation in front of him.

Would he find what he was looking for?

Or was he too late?

* * *

Evie dashed around the corner to the local internet café—dawdled, more like, in the damp heat, and went online to check her emails.

She scanned the list and pretended she wasn't hoping to see one from Zac. She was lousy at pretending. Letitia had written again, though, and from the subject heading, she had good news. Good news had been in short supply in the few weeks since Jonno's death.

'Yes!' Evie cheered. Bingo games, raffle tickets, sell-out slap-up dinners for families and friends in the nursing-home common room—including one for Nancy's 85th birthday—had exceeded expectations. Her legend of a mother, with the help of a loyal band—Zac among them, although she'd try and ignore that inclusion—had raised the funds to allow her to stay on for at least another three months. Letitia was at pains to stress it wasn't charity for Evie—Pelican Beach had rallied around the cause as a way to thank her for saving the nursing-home.

There was more, and by now she was grinning so hard she was in danger of straining something. So much had been raised that a sizeable one-off donation was also to come. Finally, an email campaign—that had to have been Letitia's doing as she didn't credit anyone in particular—circulating details of the foundation and calling for people to band together to sponsor children had resulted in pledges to sponsor at least five children.

Hitting 'Print,' she waited with impatience before heading back to the foundation. This time she went at a run, straight to Alla, the indefatigable woman whose massive task it was to oversee all fundraising and sponsorship, and vetting and placement of volunteers. She was as thrilled as Evie with the news, and enveloped her in a hug against her matronly bosom.

'I'm hearing the words "Pelican Beach" a lot nowadays. I've been trying to catch you to mention Zac Carlisle.'

'Zac? How have you heard his name?'

'More than heard his name, honey. I shook his hand not more than two hours ago. He's here and he made it clear we have you to thank for leading him to us.'

Evie sat down in the chair opposite Alla, the whir of the ceiling fan hardly audible over the ringing in her ears. She hadn't heard right—

'I was at my wits' end, trying to find a doctor for the new centre up north. I was almost at the point where we'd have to pull one of the staff from the Mekong clinic. Now you've fixed the problem and brought us Zac.'

'There must be a mistake.'

Zac couldn't be here. How could she face him? The memories of what she'd done, and said, came flooding back in full Technicolor glory. If she could have crawled under Alla's desk and howled with the excruciating agony of it all, she would have. With thousands of miles, wave upon wave of sea between them, she was getting through her days. Just. Pretence hadn't become reality but it was better. Now reality was crashing through and declaring itself present. Present and about to be accounted for.

'No mistake. He's been in, signed on and headed for his hotel. He's probably back here by now to have a look around. We'll train him up for a few weeks before shipping him up north, so to speak.' Alla was now sorting papers on her desk, talking and working simultaneously coming naturally to a woman who eked more hours out of her day than humanly possible. 'He's fine-looking. Is there nothing to tell? We need a nurse up north, too. It's an easy matter to assign you there instead.' She plopped a pile of papers on her desk and pinned Evie with a look.

'I—' Zac was here? It didn't make sense.

'I'll leave you to think about it. I haven't processed your placement yet, I was holding off until you heard about funds. I can hold off a day or two more.'

'Thanks but—'

Alla waved away what she probably thought was an expression of appreciation. It wasn't—she'd been going to say she didn't need even a minute to know she wanted to be at the opposite end of the country from Zac. He didn't even like her!

'You let me know when you're ready. I have to run, I've a meeting with the government department about visas.' Alla bustled around her desk and swept Evie along with her out the door, leaving her with a wave. Evie simply stood there with no idea what she was meant to do next.

She couldn't see him—and if he had any feelings for her at all, he'd never have come here. Steeling herself against the inevitable meeting, she returned to the medical centre, instructing herself to put one foot in front of the other and act like everything was OK. There was no room for her personal issues here, not when there was real need behind the brave faces of each one of their children.

But there he was.

She stopped as if she'd been stunned by a mallet.

She *had* been stunned.

It was definitely him. Straight back, broad shoulders, dark hair cut shorter than when she'd last seen him, but definitely him. If she wanted to believe her eyes were lying, her treacherous body wasn't letting her buy that for a minute. After everything that had happened, after every hurtful word, after recalling every morning that he didn't want her, her body hadn't learned a thing. She still wanted him.

As much as she ever had.

More?

She hung back, to watch, to see what tricks fate had in store for her. He was speaking to Carrie, the psychologist from Canada, and Shane, the GP from Melbourne. He was looking… happy? In long, lightweight trousers, a crisp white shirt that would be a nightmare to keep clean and uncreased, and leather sandals on his feet, he looked at ease. In profile, he looked thinner—or was it just the loose fit of the clothes? With the exception of the shirt—madness!—he looked like he belonged.

Which meant—what?

A doctor was always more in demand than a nurse here, harder to recruit and harder to keep. He'd trump her presence any day.

So where did that leave her?

Carrie was shaking him by the hand, Shane slapping him on the back in welcome before they went their separate ways, leaving Zac to look about.

Leaving Zac to turn straight to her, as if he'd sensed her there. Which was ridiculous.

The relaxed confidence surrounding him a moment ago ebbed almost visibly away and he hesitated before coming to her.

'Evie.' He reached out to touch her then dropped his hand when she took a step back.

'What are you doing here?' Ridiculous question. She knew what he was doing here. What she needed to know was why he had come. How could the fantastic news about the fundraising efforts be so quickly tainted with this? Why did fate have to flaunt the one thing she wanted and couldn't have in front of her like this?

He'd looked pleased to see her for a moment but the apparent joy had quickly been replaced by a smile that was less certain. She didn't know which was more confusing.

'Can we talk?' He was earnest, his voice modulated, low.

'Just tell me what you're doing here.'

'Let's grab one of those coffees you're hooked on and I'll explain.'

She didn't want to share her coffee with him.

She didn't want to share any of this with him.

This was supposed to be her safe haven but now it…wasn't safe?

Or wasn't hers?

Zac lifted his hands, imploring her to listen. 'You don't have to talk but if you'd be prepared to listen, I've got things I'd like to say. Need to say.'

'I have…' she glanced at her watch '…an hour, no more.' Once she'd had all eternity to give— but she'd offered that and he'd turned her down and left her with no doubt that the single night they'd shared had been more than enough.

Heat burned through her at the memory. If she lived to be a thousand, she'd never forget the feeling of being rejected. By this man, the one, the only man she'd ever loved.

'An hour, no more.' If she repeated it enough

she'd remember her mantra—no more. No more hurt, no more wishing, no more daydreams about a future that was never going to happen.

No more Zac Carlisle.

He'd started with an hour but the minutes were already dwindling. They'd spent five minutes walking here, to a street stall, ordered their coffee and now they were perching on two bright red plastic chairs on the potholed pavement next to the road that, considering it was a side street, was still carrying its fair share of traffic.

Watching the dark coffee drip through its aluminium filter onto the inch-thick layer of condensed milk in the glass below was like watching an egg-timer marking off the minutes until Evie blew the whistle and said, 'Game over.'

Her hair was pulled back, a light sheen on her flushed skin the only sign that she was at all affected by the dense heat of the late afternoon. She looked well, but she was tense, had been from the moment he'd seen her today, and she was watching him with wary eyes like he was a venomous creature and she was the prey.

Sitting opposite her, their glasses positioned between them like a miniature wall, he floun-

dered, and the words he'd thought would come
so easily dried up in the face of her clear wish to
be somewhere else, anywhere else other than
here with him. Where to start? With what she'd
asked him before.

'You asked me why I'm here.' She jumped as
his voice broke the silence that had fallen
between them. He was trying to make eye contact
but she was staring resolutely at her glass, seemingly mesmerised by the drip, drip, drip of the
coffee onto condensed milk. He could have sworn
she was mouthing something under her breath,
over and over again, 'No more' maybe? He was
conscious of the fascination the stall owners had
with the spectacle taking place in front of them.
What were they predicting? She'd hurl her coffee
over him any moment? Judging by the frown set
in place on her usually happy face, it was a front
runner in the list of possible outcomes.

He gave up on the eye contact.

And he gave up on trying for the perfect
formula, the perfect speech. He'd wing it. Go
with what he felt.

'There's no right place to start, there's so much
I want to say to you. So much I need to say. I
offended you in every possible way but I didn't

realise until I had hour upon hour of emptiness after you'd gone to relive every daft word I'd said, every daft thing I'd done.'

If he hadn't seen her swallow, hard, like she was fighting back her emotions, he'd have sworn she hadn't heard him. She picked up her little metal spoon and started to stir her coffee into the sweet white layer below.

'I knew within a day I had to come after you, had to apologise, even if you never wanted to see me again afterwards, but really what I wanted was to bring you home, start over. But I didn't know where you were. I ended up asking your mum and one thing led to another and there I was, involved in the fundraising, doing the exact opposite of what I wanted: raising funds to keep you here. But the more I got involved, the more I understood what it meant to you, being here.'

She snapped her head up at that, defiance in her eyes. 'If you really meant that, you wouldn't have come.' The bite in her voice was covering the hurt, but only just. How could he have so carelessly trampled over her heart then added a few extra stamps for good measure? 'Being here is everything to me but you waltz in and...' Her words were left hanging.

What was he doing here?

There was a note of desperation in her voice, in the taut carriage of her body that made him doubt, for a flicker of a moment, his right to simply launch himself into her life, this life, when he'd told her in such cruel terms to get out of his.

'I owe you an explanation. I made a lot of assumptions and they were all wrong. It's no excuse, but I was confused. Afraid. Plain stupid.'

She didn't argue the point. 'You did make a lot of assumptions but it doesn't matter now. You don't have to come and smooth things over. You wanted me out of your life, I went. So why have you come into my life here? Now?'

He could hear confusion mixed with anger in her words. Her mum, Fel, Letitia, the whole damn town had been cheering him on in his quest to come and find her once he'd announced his plans, wishing him well, reaffirming at every point he was making the right choice. The only choice. Had he glossed over how much he'd messed up?

'Please, hear me out, then if you never want to see me again, I'll respect that.'

Her nod was as grudging as it could be.

He took what he could get and pressed on. 'I've

come here for two reasons. The more I got involved in the fundraising, the more I knew there was a new path I was meant to take, whether or not you ever spoke to me again. I applied for the position up north so if you didn't want a bar of me, you wouldn't have to even know I was here.'

The stall owner chose that moment to slip their glasses away, and spoke to Evie, perhaps asking her if they wanted more. She hesitated then replied. He hadn't heard her speak Vietnamese before. She'd insisted she spoke it poorly but they seemed to be having a rapid exchange of words and a moment later the man had handed them each a baguette liberally slathered with cheese.

A baguette she showed no interest in and he knew she'd ordered them only to do the right thing by the stall owner. Yet he'd hurled it in her face that they didn't even know one another. How could he have got it all so badly wrong?

His momentum broken, he toyed with the unwanted baguette, buying time until he'd picked up his train of thought. 'If you tell me you never want to see me again, I'll go north and I promise I'll leave you be.'

Her concentration as she tore her baguette into tiny pieces was impressive but was there a flicker of indecision in her brow? A crack in her armour of self-control and containment? He wouldn't know until he'd risked as much as she had when she'd offered him everything and he'd given her nothing.

It couldn't hurt more than it already did.

'The other reason I came is this: I love you.'

Now he had not only eye contact, he had her gaping at him, incredulity clear on her face. Adrenalin surged through him—could she hear the mad pounding of his heart? 'I've loved you since the first moment I saw you shake those hips of yours.' Was that a slight, ever so slight upward twitch of that perfect mouth of hers? 'Maybe since the first moment I saw you. I fought it, God knows, and hurt you in the process. I was trying to protect myself but I've ended up hurting myself more than ever. And, worse, I've hurt you. So whether or not you give a damn, that's the second, or the first, really, the main reason I'm here. I love you and I want to be with you. For ever. And I want to share your journey here. All of it.'

She stared at him. He waited for her to speak.

Finally, she broke the silence. 'You don't like me. I'm not what you want, not who you want.

I'm not good enough.' She listed all the versions of the awful words he'd said to her all those weeks ago. The list rolled off her tongue. He knew in that moment, in a blinding flash of insight, that she'd lain awake at night hearing those hurtful, horrible words over and over in her head.

There was more.

'And you thought I was selfish, coming back here. You didn't say so, but I could see it in your eyes, in the way you behaved. You thought I was selfish to leave when Letitia was still recovering, when my mum had just arrived.'

'It was all a fiction, Evie. I thought I had to push you away, for both our sakes.' He broke into her flood of words, desperate to stem their flow and make her see how wrong he'd been. 'I'd tried explaining my reasons, reasons I thought would make you run for the hills. But you didn't. You stayed. And got tested for CF.' He shook his head at the wonder of it all. He still couldn't believe this incredible woman had done that for him. She'd risked her heart and he'd been afraid to meet her even an inch down the path, let alone halfway. 'You were brave. Wonderfully so. You made promises I just didn't, couldn't, believe were real. I was a fool.'

She'd swept the crumbs of her baguette aside and was no longer fidgeting. She was looking back at him as if he was speaking a language of which she had only a limited grasp, making comprehension a struggle. But she was listening.

'And as for why you left, I know I helped drive you away. I can't put into words all the mistakes I've made. I've spent the last two and a half months listing them all and it seemed to me that every minute we spent together, I hurt you in some way. There's no reason in the world why you should believe I love you, but I've quit my job, packed up the house and I'm here. For at least a year. And after that, who knows? But if I get what I want, whatever I'm doing, it'll be with you, wherever you want to be.'

The mask of control had been thrown aside now, replaced by the same panic and confusion he'd seen on her face when he'd spurned her love all those weeks ago. 'You don't work like that. You're not spontaneous. Sooner or later, you'll realise you don't mean any of this and then you'll go back to your old life. The one you didn't want me to be a part of.'

'Now you sound like me, fighting what's so damn obvious.' He reached out to lift her hand and she didn't resist—he couldn't even be sure she knew he'd done it. 'And you're right, I'm not spontaneous. Which is why, when loving you happened so suddenly, it terrified me. You crashed through all the barriers I'd built, turned all my reasons not to love upside down. I panicked. I did the only thing I knew how. I put up more barriers, and drove you away in the process.' He paused, brushing his hair off his forehead, unused to the sticky heat, his discomfort compounded by the desperate need he had to explain, to convince her. 'I lost my sister when she'd only just begun to be the woman she should have lived to be. I lost my daughter before she ever had a chance to live. There was nothing I could do for either of them. What was I meant to think except that love hurts like hell and promises are worthless?'

'And there you were.' He dropped his voice, the love he felt for her evident in his tone. 'Making the most incredible promises.' He pressed her fingers between his own, willing his convictions to filter through to her, to persuade her. 'I wanted so badly to believe, so very badly, but I didn't know how. So I pushed you away. But I'm here now. I'm here and I'm hoping that sometimes miracles do happen.'

His voice caught on his words and she went to tear another piece from her baguette and found her hand was in his—when had that happened? She tugged at the contact, but it was half-hearted. She wanted desperately to accept he was really here for her. But if she gave an inch, she'd end up lost in his world again. She couldn't afford to be swayed by him tugging at her heartstrings, but his sincerity was urging her better self to return his honesty.

'You're right,' she said, drawing the words out as she thought it over. 'I made all sorts of rash promises. You were right not to believe them, right to question them. I sounded insane, and I knew that by the time I arrived here. Coming back here calmed me, cleared my mind, and although I tried hard, I could no longer deny that I hadn't thought any of it through.' She hadn't met his eyes. The mortification of how she'd thrown herself at him was still too strong for that. 'I would have run a mile, too, if someone had proposed a life together and babies and moving countries to be together in the way I did.'

She felt his hand cup her face and turn it up gently. 'It sounded rash, Evie, but eventually I realised you believed what you were saying. You knew what your heart held and I was a stranger to mine. I was afraid to love because I knew it would end in more pain. I was wrong. Loving you didn't hurt, letting you go did. And letting you go, believing I didn't care, believing I didn't want you, has been indescribably terrible. I've spent the best part of the last two months hating myself and throwing myself into the fundraising as a way to stay close to you, to keep your dreams alive. And I found my new path. I've done what I could do in Pelican Beach, at least for now, but here I can make a difference. Here I can give love and care to a multitude of children, give all the things I wanted to give my daughter. And do it while being with you, loving you, sharing your dreams.'

'But your life is in Pelican Beach, your work. You're saying you'll sacrifice all that to be where I am?'

'It's not a sacrifice, it's an adventure, but it's one I've thought through. I'm not asking for an answer now. I'm asking you to give me a chance. You showed me there are many paths to love and if you're lucky enough to stumble on your true path, you seize it. This is our path, our adventure. Take this path with me, Evie. Trust me. Love me, like I love you.'

Frantically, she searched her mind for all remaining obstacles. There was one, but when he
was looking at her like that it was all she could
do not to give in.

They should go. They should walk. Walking
would clear her head. Walking would mean he
couldn't look at her like that, as if she was his world.
Because that was exactly what she wanted to be.

And there was one more obstacle that couldn't
be easily swept aside. One more hurdle that
might still be too high.

He'd thought she was about to close the distance
between them and when she stood, his heart
expanded to fill every corner of his chest. But she
lifted her little red chair out the way and said,
'Can we walk? Please?'

He followed suit with his chair and thanked
the stall owner, using the few words he'd learnt
from his language book, and walked beside her
along the street. Her posture was rigid.
Something was still bothering her.

'What's wrong?'

'Children,' was all she said, her voice a whisper.
'You were right. I want—need—to know
children are in my future.'

'We can't have children. I can't take the risk of a child having CF.'

She turned away. He touched her arm, turning her to him, and his heart caught in his throat at the expression of pain on her face.

'You spoke about adoption. Is that still what you would do, what is really in your heart?'

She nodded.

'That was the final dream of yours I had to be certain I could share with as much conviction and passion and love as you.'

'And can you?'

'Yes.'

Hope and joy flared in her eyes for a brief moment before clouds came into her expression again. 'Do you really know that's right for you? It's a long, intrusive, demanding path to travel. You have no idea how much prodding and poking you have to endure from officials, how much assessment and paperwork and red tape you'd face. And it's necessary, to ensure everything is aboveboard and the child who'll eventually become your son or daughter has no options in their birth country other than growing up in an institution, often in immense poverty. I couldn't go down this path with you if it's all going to come crashing down when reality hits.'

'This isn't a spur-of-the-moment decision, it's another reason why I had to wait to come to you. I wanted no doubts between us. I've spent every possible minute looking into this. I needed to be sure it was what I wanted before I came sailing back into your life on a raft of promises I couldn't keep. I've been to information nights and seminars and group workshops and trawled the internet and libraries for information. My friends and family think I've joined some secret men's club in Adelaide because I've disappeared so often.'

Her eyes were huge, their expression hovering somewhere between incredulity and excitement, her lips parted, hanging on his every word.

'I've met wonderful families and seen the love they have for their children. They've formed their families via another path but the love is the same. This is not only what I want but where I'm meant to be.'

'You did all that for me? For us?'

'It's the tip of the iceberg. There's nothing I wouldn't do to have the future I dream of with you. You're my future, Evie. Let me love you, let me show you what you mean to me.'

A sob tore from her throat and he resisted the urge to gather her to him, comfort her when she might still pull away. He needed to convince her. There were still things left to say.

'And one day there will be a child who was meant to have you for his mother, whose chubby little arms were meant to wrap tight around you, whose dimpled baby hands were made to stroke your face.' A single tear slid down her cheek but she made no effort to brush it away, if she even felt it. 'He, or she, is real, Evie. I can almost feel our child, and one day it will happen.'

He was done. He'd said what he'd needed to say. He took her in his arms and for the first time since he'd arrived she let him hold her. They stood there, body to body, heart to heart. And he let himself hope.

He'd seen almost every emotion under the sun in her face today and he'd thought, hoped he'd seen love among them.

'Come with me to the northern clinic—there are places for both of us. Give me the chance to show you how I feel, give us the chance to start again.'

She shook her head. 'No.'

His world stopped. 'No?'

She raised her face to look into his eyes and her gaze was at odds with her words. 'No chances. You don't need a chance.' Her smile was radiant. It was all for him. 'I believe you,' she added simply as if that was enough.

Maybe it was.

'You believe me,' he said. 'Enough to trust me? Enough to let me love you?'

'Enough for all of that and more. Enough to love you back. I've never stopped, I've wished I could, many, many times, because that would have ended the pain, but love doesn't work like that.'

'Thank God for me.' He lifted her up then and kissed her, kissed her with every ounce of love he had, and the kiss was everything he'd ever hoped, everything that had kept him tossing and turning through endless sleepless nights these past two months.

All his love and dreams and passion were in that kiss.

And in his arms, kissing him back as though they were the only two people on the planet, was the woman he loved more than life itself.

When they drew apart, minutes later, she whispered, 'I thought wild horses wouldn't drag this out of me after how it went down last time, but I love you, Zac Carlisle. And I will love you every minute of every day for the rest of my life.'

'Only the days? What about the nights?'

'Especially the nights.' She reached up for him again, kissing him once more, more gently this time but with just as much passion. 'And that's a promise.'

A promise.

How could he ever have thought promises brought trouble?

Promises had brought him Evie.

Which left him in no doubt at all that some promises were, in fact, for ever.

PS

MEDICAL™

Large Print

Titles for the next six months…

May

THE MAGIC OF CHRISTMAS	Sarah Morgan
THEIR LOST-AND-FOUND FAMILY	Marion Lennox
CHRISTMAS BRIDE-TO-BE	Alison Roberts
HIS CHRISTMAS PROPOSAL	Lucy Clark
BABY: FOUND AT CHRISTMAS	Laura Iding
THE DOCTOR'S PREGNANCY BOMBSHELL	Janice Lynn

June

CHRISTMAS EVE BABY	Caroline Anderson
LONG-LOST SON: BRAND-NEW FAMILY	Lilian Darcy
THEIR LITTLE CHRISTMAS MIRACLE	Jennifer Taylor
TWINS FOR A CHRISTMAS BRIDE	Josie Metcalfe
THE DOCTOR'S VERY SPECIAL CHRISTMAS	Kate Hardy
A PREGNANT NURSE'S CHRISTMAS WISH	Meredith Webber

July

THE ITALIAN'S NEW-YEAR MARRIAGE WISH	Sarah Morgan
THE DOCTOR'S LONGED-FOR FAMILY	Joanna Neil
THEIR SPECIAL-CARE BABY	Fiona McArthur
THEIR MIRACLE CHILD	Gill Sanderson
SINGLE DAD, NURSE BRIDE	Lynne Marshall
A FAMILY FOR THE CHILDREN'S DOCTOR	Dianne Drake

MILLS & BOON®
Pure reading pleasure

0408 LP 2P P1 Medical

MEDICAL™

Large Print

August

THE DOCTOR'S BRIDE BY SUNRISE	Josie Metcalfe
FOUND: A FATHER FOR HER CHILD	Amy Andrews
A SINGLE DAD AT HEATHERMERE	Abigail Gordon
HER VERY SPECIAL BABY	Lucy Clark
THE HEART SURGEON'S SECRET SON	Janice Lynn
THE SHEIKH SURGEON'S PROPOSAL	Olivia Gates

September

THE SURGEON'S FATHERHOOD SURPRISE	Jennifer Taylor
THE ITALIAN SURGEON CLAIMS HIS BRIDE	Alison Roberts
DESERT DOCTOR, SECRET SHEIKH	Meredith Webber
A WEDDING IN WARRAGURRA	Fiona Lowe
THE FIREFIGHTER AND THE SINGLE MUM	Laura Iding
THE NURSE'S LITTLE MIRACLE	Molly Evans

October

THE DOCTOR'S ROYAL LOVE-CHILD	Kate Hardy
HIS ISLAND BRIDE	Marion Lennox
A CONSULTANT BEYOND COMPARE	Joanna Neil
THE SURGEON BOSS'S BRIDE	Melanie Milburne
A WIFE WORTH WAITING FOR	Maggie Kingsley
DESERT PRINCE, EXPECTANT MOTHER	Olivia Gates

™ MILLS & BOON®

Pure reading pleasure

0408 LP 2P P2 Medical